Also by **Jane St. Anthony**

The Summer Sherman Loved Me

Grace
Above All

Grace
Above All

Jane St. Anthony

Farrar Straus Giroux • *New York*

www.fsgkidsbooks.com

Library of Congress Cataloging-in-Publication Data
St. Anthony, Jane.
     Grace above all / Jane St. Anthony.— 1st ed.
        p.   cm.
     Summary: When thirteen-year-old Grace, her mother, and four siblings go
to her mother's childhood cabin by a lake over the summer, as usual Grace
is in charge of all the kids while her mother does nothing, but after meeting
some relatives Grace becomes a bit more understanding, and learns to
stand up for herself.
     ISBN-13: 978-0-374-39940-5
     ISBN-10: 0-374-39940-9
     [1. Mothers—Fiction.   2. Family life—Fiction.   3. Vacations—Fiction.
4. Interpersonal relations—Fiction.]   I. Title.

PZ7.S1413 Gr 2007
[Fic]—dc22

                                                           2006047630

For my mother and father, Jane and Paul,
for my brothers, Paul and Neal,
and
for my sister, Ann

Grace
Above All

The morning sun streaked through the cobwebbed porch windows into the big room. On the rollaway, Grace squinted, then turned her face from the brightness. Across the expanse, her brother Chuck lay curled on the daybed, his back to Grace. Grace winced. Today began almost two weeks of summer vacation that would be wasted at this cabin with Bernadette and the kids, although Dad would enliven the weekend.

Squeezing her eyes shut, Grace pictured her friend Margaret in the city. Margaret's day would begin as soon as she finished her mother's job list. Here there would be no escape. Job list? Her life was a job list.

Rubbing one eye with her fingers, six-year-old Beth emerged from the hallway into the main room, a jumble of sofas and recliners, a dining table, and the disguisable beds occupied by Grace and Chuck. The refrigerator, sink, stove, and doorway to the bedrooms shared one wall. When the family had arrived after dark the night before,

Bernadette sent Beth as well as Polly and Pinky through that doorway to one of the two real bedrooms. Bernadette commandeered the other.

Grace shut her eyes again. She wasn't fast enough.

"Will you take me swimming, Gracie?" Beth asked. The family baby was a timid, smaller version of Grace, complete with a strawberry blond ponytail that drooped after a night in bed.

"Bernadette will take you when she gets up."

"What did you say, Gracie?"

"Mom will take you when she gets up."

"Oh," said Beth, already dressed in a pink-skirted swimsuit. She dragged her "Oh" out softly, easing into a long sigh. Grace worried that Beth might turn out to be a freak, the kind of kid who printed her letters backward and stared at people as if she couldn't understand them.

"I'm still sleeping."

"But you're talking to me, Gracie."

"I was sleeping. I'm going back to sleep now."

Grace opened one eye and watched her sister disappear onto the porch. She heard Beth settle into a wicker chair.

A door closed within the hallway. Bernadette surfaced at the same spot Beth had occupied moments earlier. Her floral orange-and-red shift was as wrinkled as it would be if it had been wadded up under her pillow. She frowned into the sunlight.

"Two bodies accounted for in the bedroom. Did we lose Bethie already?" Bernadette paused to flip open her silver cigarette lighter and start her day with smoke.

"She's out there," Grace said, lifting her face from the pillow, hand gesturing at the porch. Pretending to be asleep was pointless.

Beth appeared in the doorway. "Mommy, may I go swimming?"

"What's all the noise?" groaned Chuck from his bed as he pulled a sheet over his head.

"Jeez, Bethie, I'd like a cup of java before I go on patrol," Bernadette said, banging cupboard doors as she searched for coffee. "Finally." She plucked a can from the shelf.

"Mommy, may I go swimming?"

"Let me wake up first," Bernadette said, her hand crashing around in a drawer. "You would think she owned a can opener."

"Who owned a can opener?" said Chuck.

"Aunt Marie, you idiot," Grace answered. At fifteen, Chuck was two years older than Grace and, Grace thought, about a century dumber. "This was her cabin."

"Oh, yeah, Grandma's dead sister."

"Gad, did they bury it with her?" said Bernadette, finally extracting her prize from the drawer, which she shut with her hip. She positioned the can opener's little cutting wheel and turned the handle.

"Mommy, maybe?" Beth's gentle voice floated from the doorway.

"What's for breakfast?" Chuck demanded loudly.

"That's an original question," Bernadette said. "Am I supposed to turn into a waffle iron because you're on vacation?" She pulled a *Good Housekeeping* magazine out of a stack piled on a shelf built into the wall. The fire hissed under the coffeepot.

Even though the sun was heating the cabin, Grace slipped deeper under the bedspread for privacy. She wondered whether Bernadette had bought hot dog buns. She didn't remember seeing them when she had unpacked the grocery bags last night. Hot dogs wrapped in Wonder Bread were hateful.

"Are there any bikes up here?" Grace asked. The last town they had driven through couldn't be too far away, could it?

"Never were a hundred years ago when I was here last," Bernadette said.

The coffee began to perk on the stove, the water beating against the little glass dome.

"Keep things under control, Gracie," Bernadette called back as she disappeared into the hallway. "I'll be back for my brew." The bedroom door clicked shut.

"Please, may I go swimming now?" Beth asked quietly.

Grace sat up on the rollaway. She would never get back to sleep.

"Go on, Bethie, but only up to your knees. Got it? Just up to your knees. I'll be out in a minute."

The screen door squeaked open and bounced shut a few times. Beth's bare feet padded away from the cabin.

The old linoleum floor was cool under Grace's soles as she walked to the cupboard where she had put the cereal. At least Bernadette had remembered to buy that before they had left home. Grace looked through the cupboards, memorizing the location of anything that might be useful. Picking up an eggbeater from the utensil drawer, Grace absentmindedly turned the handle. A spider dropped from between the blades and scooted away.

Polly walked into the big room, bumping into an end table as she blinked in the brightness.

"Having trouble walking, Polly?" Chuck muttered.

"At least I'm not paralyzed, fathead," Polly shot back as she rubbed her shin. She stopped to peer through the porch into the sun. Polly was the most nearsighted twelve-year-old—or kid, for that matter—that Grace knew.

"What's that pink thing out there?" Polly said, squinting hard.

"Maybe your brain went for a swim," said Chuck.

Polly put her face up to the window and strained to see through the porch.

"Grace, is that a person?"

Why me? Grace thought. You don't have a mother?

She walked away from the cupboards and stood next to Polly. "Where?" she asked.

"There, floating, I think."

Grace looked at Polly. She wasn't wearing her glasses. She really couldn't see what she saw. Grace's chest seized with panic.

"Can't you see it, Grace? Pink."

Think, think, think, Grace repeated to herself. No lifeguard here. Who else could swim besides her? Bernadette, no. Chuck, yes, but not as well as she could. Polly, slow dog paddle. Pinky, no. Maybe Chuck could float on something. She moved quickly to Chuck's head, which had emerged from the sheet. Grace put her mouth next to his ear.

"Keep your fat trap shut," she said in a hissing whisper. "Beth is floating on something in the middle of the lake. We're going to get her. Now."

"Get Mom," Chuck said in a strained voice.

"She can't swim. She'll slow us down."

Chuck stood up in his T-shirt and boxers.

"We're going down to the beach to check out the situation, Pol," Grace called as she ran through the porch and let the screen door slam. Chuck followed, pushing the door open behind her and following down the steps to the beach. The door bounced in protest again.

At the bottom of the steps, the cool sand shocked Grace.

A weather-beaten rowboat floated next to the dock,

joined to it by rope. Should she hunt for paddles under the junk heaped in the boat? How hard would it be to untie it? Grace decided. No time. She had to act.

"What should we do?" Chuck asked.

"Grab that inner tube. I'll swim."

"Where's the tube?"

Grace gestured toward the adjoining beachfront as she moved to the water.

"Too hard to swim with a tube," Chuck protested.

"We need it. Do it."

For a second, Grace marveled that her older brother obeyed her in times of crisis. Dad said that she was born to be a military commander. As a toddler, she had barked orders: "Make food!" "Push higher!" "Move, Chuckie!"

From the cabin, the unmistakable high voice of Pinky, their younger brother, shot down to the beach.

"Bethie's in the lake!" he screamed. "Mom, Bethie's in the lake!"

2

Grace plunged. She forced her arms to chop through the water as if she might escape its cold grip. Chuck yelped behind her as he splashed into the lake. How far out was Beth? Grace tried to gauge the distance in regulation-size swimming pools. Three pools? Four? More?

A few fishing boats perched in the distance, the fishermen minuscule on the sun-dappled lake. As Grace swam toward her, Beth became more distinct, gently bobbing on an air mattress—the kind that some moms floated around on in shallow water and then yelled at their kids from when they got splashed. Afraid of losing time, Grace lifted her face completely out of the water to right her course only every few breaths. She hadn't given the lake a thought earlier. Now the water lapped a little—hitting her face with insulting little slaps—but at least a hurricane wasn't flipping wave walls at her. She would trade Chuck for a pair of goggles. Where was he, anyway? What was she, the world's lifeguard?

Beth began to turn her head slowly as Grace closed in on her. The air mattress submerged where Beth's hand pushed on it as she tried to look back and balance at the same time.

"Turn around," Grace called. "Don't move, Bethie." Could Chuck be catching up on the inner tube? The splashing came closer. Grace hated to waste energy by yelling at Beth again. Lake swimming was so much more work than pool swimming. The Girl Scouts should have been dumped in the middle of a lake instead of taking lessons in that smooth chlorinated bath at the junior high.

From far away on the beach, a muddle of voices reached her across the water. If Grace had waited for someone else to figure out what to do, Beth would have floated to Canada by now. That was, if the air mattress didn't deflate. Whose was it, anyway, all puffed up, luring little kids onto it?

For every splash Grace made, a splash echoed. Grace pushed forward, focused on Beth's ponytail rather than on the depth of the lake. When Grace pulled alongside her sister, Beth's slurpy crying burbled over the water. Grace gently held the lip of the air mattress, taking care to move slowly for fear of jostling the rider. She didn't want Beth on her neck.

"Hey, Bethie," she said. "Pretty out here, isn't it?" Grace held on to an edge of Beth's boat and kicked her feet to stay afloat. The lake was friendlier now.

Beth looked past Grace at the swimmer who had splashed up. "Who is it, Gracie?" she said, voice still stiff with fright.

Grace turned to see a wet head bobbing next to her, and a life jacket trailing by its belt. For a second it seemed that Chuck had turned into someone handsome.

"The other guy was falling back, so I took over," the boy said. "I can tow the little girl on the flotation thing. You take this. You really raced out here."

"Okay," Grace said as she struggled into the life jacket. "Here we go, Bethie. You're getting a ride."

"Let's go," said the handsome person who wasn't Chuck. He held on to the mattress.

"Gracie, you pull me," Beth said, tears streaming down her face.

"I'm right here, Bethie. We're all going to the same place."

Grace paced her strokes to match the boy's, slowed by the cargo. Buoyed by the life jacket, she noticed what she hadn't seen on the trip out. The sun, still climbing, heated her head. Birds called to one another. Cabins, widely spaced, peeked from behind birch and pine trees. The trip was a glide over the surface, not a struggle to stay on top.

In the distance, tiny figures peopled the beach, some cavorting, some unwavering as tree trunks. Grace picked Chuck out of the lineup as she neared the shore. He was such a fathead that he could probably float forever. She would have to tell him that.

Bernadette, bright as a field of poppies, stood out, too. Chuck jumped up and down next to her. Polly held Pinky's hands as the eight-year-old pulled her around in circles. Two men stood a little apart from Bernadette. One wore a straw hat.

"That's the way, Frankie," called the straw hat, who looked old as Grace got close enough to stand up.

"Go on, Grandpa," said the boy. Now Grace knew his name.

Grace stepped onto dry land and turned to help Frankie with the air mattress as if they were beaching a canoe. She looked Chuck in the eye. He stopped jumping.

"Afraid of sharks?" Grace asked him.

"We traded places. That guy had a life jacket."

"Bethie, Bethie, what in the blank were you trying to do?" Bernadette said in her hoarse morning voice. She scooped Beth up and held her in her arms, turning Beth into an elongated baby. Bernadette sounded like Bernadette, but the little scar on her chin was more apparent than usual in her pale face.

"The pillow floated," Beth said softly, tears squeezing out of her eyes and onto the sand. "I jumped on it to catch it. I didn't go in over my knees, Gracie."

"That's brilliant," said Chuck.

"Unlike you," Grace replied, without pause. She wished that she had a towel. The T-shirt she had slept in clung to her chest. She folded her arms over it.

"A most admirable rescue," said the straw-hat man to Grace. "My name is Ernest Hale, and I'm happy to make your acquaintance." "Grace Doyle," said Grace as Frankie's grandpa extended his dry hand and she shook it with her clammy one, leaving her left arm in place on her chest.

"Bernadette," Ernest Hale continued, including everyone with a sweep of his eyes. "It's been too many years. You remember my son, Tom. And the other swimmer is my grandson, Frankie, who just turned fourteen."

"Mr. Hale, I would know you anywhere," Bernadette said. "And you, too, Tom." She shifted Beth's weight in her arms. "Bethie, your big sister saved you. You are one lucky baby girl."

"That boy saved me, too," Beth said, her lip quivering.

"Don't cry now," said Chuck. "You've been saved."

Bernadette pulled a pack of cigarettes out of her shift pocket as she balanced Beth on her left hip. She tapped a cigarette into the hand that held Beth's bottom. "She's relieved, Chuck." She turned to the elder Mr. Hale. "First off, I'm still Bernie to you, Mr. Hale."

"Well, then, Bernie, I'm Ernest to you now."

"Okay, Ernest, we're both grownups. Whew. What a morning. Bethie, no more crazy stuff."

"And these are your other children?" asked Ernest Hale.

"Oops, my manners," Bernadette said. "This is my first-born, Chuck. That's Grace, but she already told you. That's

Polly, then Pinky, and you must have figured out that Beth is the wave rider."

"A pleasure to meet you all," said Frankie's grandpa. His son, Frankie's dad, nodded and smiled at everyone.

"And thanks to you for hauling the girls in," Bernadette said to Frankie.

"Really, she"—he looked at Grace—"was doing it by herself. I was backup. She's a good swimmer."

Grace stared at Frankie. Water dripped down his smooth chest. She wondered where he had thrown his shirt. Did the Hales have a cabin on this shore?

As if reading her mind, Grandpa Ernest pointed to a cabin mostly hidden by the trees. "Our cabin is next door to your family's," he said, looking at Grace. "We go back a long way. You must come over and visit us while you're here."

Grace was grateful for Grandpa Ernest. Staring at Frankie Hale made her weak. The strength came back to her legs. She could exit.

"Great," she said. "Thanks."

She gave a little wave and started up the wooden stairs to the cabin, although she couldn't imagine what she would do when she got there.

3

Beth sat at the head of the table, drowning in Bernadette's terry-cloth robe. In spite of the heat, Bernadette had put Beth in a steamy bath and swaddled her in the bathrobe.

"Let's go outside and play," said Pinky, who shared the title "Most Quiet" with Beth. His request was ignored.

Bernadette reached into a cupboard and pulled out a snack pack of sugared cereals.

"Hey, Mom, you made breakfast after all," Chuck said.

Feeling sorry for Pinky, Grace addressed her little brother. "Pinky, you can go out after you have something to eat, okay?" He didn't need permission but, after Beth's excursion, Grace didn't think he should roam around by himself so soon.

Grace looked at the clock. It was only nine forty-five. She had already rescued her little sister. She knew that a boy named Frankie was staying at the cabin next door. What would she do with the rest of the day?

Polly looked up from her Sugar Pops. "Let's play cards after breakfast," she said.

"That's an evening activity," Grace said.

"As if you've ever been at a cabin in your life," said Chuck, who had been drinking milk from the bottom of his cereal bowl.

"I know these things," Grace answered, drumming her fingers on the wooden tabletop. "You play cards in the evening. You swim in the afternoon."

"What do you do in the morning?" Polly asked.

Grace dug around in her brain for an answer. "You walk into town for supplies."

"What supplies?" said Chuck.

"You know, snacks. Hot dog buns."

No one seemed to know whether or not this was a fact of cabin life.

"Ma," Chuck ventured, eyeing Grace with suspicion, "how far is that town we came through?"

"I don't know anymore," Bernadette said as she filled a thermos with coffee. "Maybe six, seven miles."

"So much for swimming this afternoon," Chuck said. "You'll be walking all day."

Grace did the math. One mile, about twenty minutes. Six miles, two hours. Add a little for Bernadette's underestimating. "Most people build cabins closer to town than this so that they can walk for supplies when the roads aren't clear," she said.

"So it's the cabin's fault that we can't walk to town and back in the morning?" asked Polly.

"No, it's Grace's fault for making things up," Chuck said.

"Forget it," said Grace. "Don't come to me when you've all died of boredom by lunchtime." She glared at Polly. "Go hang out with Chuck if you don't like my ideas."

"Come on, Grace, tell us what to do," Polly pleaded. "Just tell us what to do if we're not going to walk into town."

"Well," Grace said, rolling her eyes. "I had no idea we would be cut off from civilization. Let's move on to another plan."

"A lemonade stand?" suggested Beth.

"Great idea," Chuck said. "There's so much traffic out here."

Grace reached into her memory and saw the bag of bruised lemons that she had carried to the car yesterday. Mr. Waltham, their next-door neighbor at home, managed a grocery store and regularly offered Bernadette the past-its-prime produce.

"That is a great idea, Bethie. We'll make lemonade for the Hales. We'll say it's a thank-you for helping save you this morning.

"Bernadette, did you bring the lemon squeezer?" Grace called through the open porch window to where her mother had moved with the thermos and a pile of magazines.

"No, but there's one in the cupboard where the coffee was, over the sink," Bernadette called back.

"Polly, get that squeezer and look for a strainer," Grace ordered. "And measuring cups. And sugar. And pitchers."

Polly folded her arms across her chest. "What are you going to do?"

"Pol, get cracking. I am the recipe. Two to three lemons per half cup of sugar. Et cetera. Let's go."

Polly squeezed the lemons because she was stronger than Pinky or Beth. Pinky carefully poured the lemon juice into the strainer that Beth held solemnly over the pitcher. Grace measured the sugar.

"Chuck, get the ice," Grace ordered. "We'll reduce the water and add cubes so it's cold."

"I tried to get the trays out last night. They were stuck to the freezer."

"Pinky," Grace said, "go help Chuck get the ice cube trays out."

"I'll do it, I'll do it," Chuck grumbled, getting up from his chair.

The lemons yielded two full pitchers plus a little extra that Grace saved in a saucepan.

"Beth and I will take a pitcher over now," Grace said, choosing the one that didn't have as many nicks in the glass.

"I'm going, too," said Chuck.

"You are not. This is about Beth and me."

"I don't want to go," Beth said, looking alarmed.

"The lemonade is from *us*, Bethie." Grace imagined Frankie appearing at his door and inviting her in. Her stomach was Butterfly Central.

"We made the lemonade, too," Polly said.

"Next time, your show. We'll be right back."

Grace and Beth walked through long grass that tickled their bare feet and ankles. The grass in front of the Hales' cabin was newly cropped by a push mower that rested in the shade of a tilting pine.

Grace knocked on the screen door. A chair scraped the floor in response. Footsteps advanced. Grace's stomach lurched. Mr. Tom Hale, Frankie's dad, opened the door.

"Hello. What can I do for you young ladies?"

"We made lemonade because we had a lot of lemons," said Grace, aware of stating the obvious. "It's a thank-you to Frankie for the rescue this morning."

"You're looking well," Frankie's dad said to Beth. He faced Grace. "The lemonade looks great. Frankie and my dad are out trolling. We'll have some of this when they get back."

"Okay, then. See you."

"See you," Beth whispered so softly that only Grace heard.

Grace and Beth backtracked through the clipped grass to taller grass. Grace felt as if she had gone to a birthday party and left the gift without going inside. What had she expected? That Frankie would be watching for her at the window? She wanted to hide in her room, but she didn't have one.

On the porch, Bernadette stood up and stretched. "After lunch, we're going into town to see Hilda and Gunda," she announced. "We should go visit them a couple of times as long as we're up here."

"I can't go," Chuck replied. He sat at the table in front of a pile of little cereal boxes. "My stomach hurts."

Grace rolled her eyes.

"We're all going," Bernadette said.

"Really, Ma, I think I have the stomach flu or something."

"The stomach flu you got from eating until you're full up to your fat face," Grace said.

"Okay, okay. It'll be easier if you two aren't at each other's throats," said Bernadette. "Chuck, you can stay here, but you're on next time."

"I just want to lie down."

Grace glared at Chuck as he smirked behind Bernadette's back.

"Do those people have any children?" Pinky asked.

Grace looked at him. Pinky was the palest of her siblings, the blue veins under his eyes apparent through the milky skin. Why wasn't his nickname Bluey?

"Jeez, no," said Bernadette. "Gunda is Hilda's kid, but she's older than me. Gunda isn't right in the head. But Hilda is Grandma's sister, so we gotta go."

"Who?" Chuck said.

"Dang it, Chuck. Whose kid are you? We covered this on the way up here. Hilda is my aunt. Her kid is Gunda, my cousin."

"Whose cabin is this?"

"Moron," Grace mouthed at him.

"Chuck, wake up," said Bernadette. "Who built this joint? I told you."

"Grandpa Olav?" Chuck answered.

"*My* Grandpa Olav. Who did he build it for?"

"You?"

"I wasted my breath," she said, blowing smoke out of her nose. "Gracie, who did my grandpa build this cabin for?"

"His three daughters. Our grandma. Aunt Hilda, who we're going to see. And Aunt Marie."

"Right," said Bernadette, walking to the refrigerator and looking inside. She reached in for a can of pop. "Why is it mine now, Gracie?"

"Grandma died a long time ago. Aunt Marie lived in the cabin during the summer, but she died last year. Aunt Hilda never wanted the cabin, and you're the only kid from those three sisters. Except for Gunda."

What would Aunt Marie think about her niece,

who had inherited the cabin? Would she like the way Bernadette looked when she wore her red bandanna that matched her red, red lips, or the pedal pushers so tight that her underpants line showed?

"Aunt Marie was nervous around kids," Bernadette said through a big puff of smoke. "I brought you and Chuck up here before Polly was born, Gracie. Marie couldn't relax."

"Why doesn't Gunda get some cabin time?" Chuck asked.

"Bernadette just told you," said Grace. "Gunda never grew up. Something's wrong in her head." A long time ago Grace had seen a picture of Gunda. It was disturbing.

Bernadette moved in the direction of her bedroom. She paused in front of Grace and looked serious. It didn't suit her.

"Gracie, thanks for watching out for Bethie."

"It's my job." But Beth had floated away because she, Grace, had given her permission to go in the lake.

"Right." Bernadette tapped a long ash onto Jefferson's face in the Mount Rushmore ashtray that sat on the countertop.

"But it shouldn't be my job." For the first time, the enormity of her decision to let Beth go struck Grace with force.

Bernadette turned and laughed without smiling. "I wish you wouldn't give me so much grief, Gracie. Lighten up."

A life-and-death decision, left up to her. If Bernadette accused Grace of negligence, she accused herself as well. Grace turned her back on Bernadette, sat down at the table, and pulled Beth's tablet with the lined paper to her. She picked up the pencil and, to quell her anger, began to calculate how long it would take her to walk home.

*

*

*I*n town, Bernadette pulled up in front of a dark gray house that almost abutted the sidewalk. A thin strip of matted brown grass fronted it and spread around the sides.

"I don't like the way this house looks," said Pinky, who worried about almost everything. He rolled up his window as if to protect himself.

"We can wait outside for you," Polly said to Bernadette. "We'll be right here when you come out."

"Maybe it's the wrong place," Pinky said, face pressed to the window.

"Let's go," said Bernadette, sliding out of the driver's seat. "C'mon, Pinky. Bethie, you, too."

"Did you tell her we're coming?" Grace asked, opening the back door slowly.

"Hilda never had a phone. If she has one now, it's news to me."

Everyone lined up behind Bernadette, with Grace at the end behind Polly.

"Hey, Pol, at least I can get away if she comes out swinging an ax," Grace said.

"This is the worst vacation I've ever had," Polly said.

"What do you mean, the worst? We've never had *any*."

"When I have children, I'll take them to Disneyland every year."

Grace thought of telling Polly that her children wouldn't like her anyway. Polly was such an easy target. Chuck had a thick hide. Pinky and Beth were too innocent. It was a waste of time to spar with Bernadette. She always turned it back on you.

Bernadette knocked a second time, causing Polly to recoil and suck in her breath. The door creaked open.

"Hilda, it's Bernadette. I brought some company for you," Bernadette blared at the slight figure wearing a bib apron. "A carful of bad children."

"Oh, my goodness," a thin voice replied. "Bernadette and her babies."

"If you let us in, you'll see there isn't a baby in the bunch. Just big, spoiled kids." Bernadette crossed the threshold, towing Beth with her. Pinky followed stiffly. Grace pushed Polly from behind. Polly didn't try to swat Grace's arms away because she needed her own hands to shield herself from whatever might be inside the house.

Hilda stood in the center of the living room as everyone filed in. Lined with two rockers and a variety of stuffed chairs, the room seemed to harbor invisible people. A shudder raced down Grace's spine.

Seen from the side, Hilda's body looked as if it were trying to make an upside-down U. The hump in her back forced her trunk to curve downward. Her head resembled a turtle's, peeking up out of its shell.

"Sit down, please sit down," said Hilda.

"Where's Gunda?" Bernadette asked, dropping into a plump chair.

"She takes a little nap after lunch. She's in her bedroom."

"Lunch. We forgot all about it."

"I have crackers," Hilda said. "I'll get some crackers for the children."

She started toward the kitchen area at the back of the house, then stopped and turned around. "I want to take a good look at the children first, Bernadette. You sent a photograph a few years ago. I don't see your oldest boy."

"Chuck isn't here. Grace is the oldest one in this bunch."

Grace moved her hand up to shoulder height and wiggled her fingers at Hilda. The rest of her didn't seem to work.

"That's Polly, then Pinky, then Beth." Bernadette pointed at her children, none of whom moved or uttered a word.

"They're lovely children, Bernadette, lovely children." Hilda smiled so that her wrinkles deepened. "Now I'll go get those crackers."

She moved slowly to the little kitchen. The living room, tiny dining area, and kitchen ran together as one large room. The two closed doors on the left side of the house must be the bedrooms, Grace guessed, and Gunda occupied one of them. Illuminated at the back window, Hilda could be seen as she peered at the countertop covered with canisters and tins.

I can't breathe, Grace thought. Was it Hilda or the smells of cabbage and lotion mingling in the heat?

"You're a little more stooped than I remember," Bernadette called to Hilda. "But you're moving around pretty good."

Stooped? Was Bernadette blind? The woman was flat-out crooked.

"I do just fine," Hilda called back. "I'm very fortunate to have my health."

What if Hilda talked to her? Grace would have to crouch to make eye contact. Hilda returned, bearing a dinner plate piled with saltines and slices of cheese.

"Please, children, sit down," Hilda said. "Help yourself to some crackers." Hilda's turtle head paused in front of Grace, who had seated herself in a rocker.

"Would you like a cracker, dear?" she said. Hilda had a sweet, coaxing smile and a knot of gray hair, which unfortunately was in the wrong position at the back of her head.

"Yes, thank you," replied Grace, wondering if taking one cracker from the plate would throw Hilda off balance.

Polly, Pinky, and Beth each took a cracker and a piece of cheese from Hilda, who put the plate on a hassock.

"So, how's things?" Bernadette said, leaning over and scooping up a handful of saltines.

"Can we play outside?" Polly squeaked in an unrecognizable voice before Hilda could answer Bernadette.

"Oh, yes, let them play outside," said Hilda. "I don't have very much for children to do in here. They seem to be such very nice children."

"They're okay some days. Go outside if you want to, kids. Don't stray, especially you, Bethie. Don't float away on me again."

Everyone crowded behind Grace, who tugged at the door a couple of times before it opened.

"I'm not going back in there," said Polly after she had pulled the door shut. "It's too weird."

"Do you ever go out in the world?" Grace asked. "Are you afraid of people just because they're old?"

"Grace, you know it's scary in there. Everything smells funny. I think I smelled liniment."

"Polly, you wouldn't know what liniment smelled like if you stepped in it."

Pinky and Beth lowered themselves to the ground, listening and quietly placing little sticks in the sidewalk cracks.

"What is liniment?" Beth asked.

"It's something that old people put on their skin," said Grace.

"That's hand lotion," Pinky said.

"It's a lotion with medicine in it for sore bones and things," Grace continued. "I saw some at Margaret's grandma's house. It looked like colored Vaseline."

"I bet you fifty cents that there's liniment in there," said Polly.

"Hurry up, then, and find it. Bernadette isn't going to camp here."

"I don't want to come back," said Pinky. "Next time I'm going fishing with Chuck."

Why was Pinky the only one who had thought of fishing? Grace didn't mention that Chuck hated having Pinky tag along.

"Here's an idea. Don't tell Chuck what it's like. Let him think that he wants to come here with Bernadette."

Polly was quiet for a moment. Then she said, "Grace, you're mean to me."

"Just some of the time. I'm meaner to Chuck."

"I want to give you a compliment, but you don't deserve it."

"What compliment?"

"Your idea about not telling is so good."

"Polly, you have potential."

"Grace—" Polly began.

"No no no. You're going to get sentimental on me. Leave it alone."

Pinky and Beth stared at their sisters as if trying to decode the conversation.

"What about them?" Polly asked, nodding at Pinky and Beth.

"I'll take care of them. I understand the junior set. You have a mission."

"What?"

"Liniment. I dare you. It's worth fifty cents."

"Please don't dare me, Grace. How am I going to look around when Mom and that Hilda are in there?"

"It's about two hundred degrees in that place. There must be an open window. If they haven't cracked one, they'll roast soon."

Polly looked defiant. "Okay, okay, I'll go look." She glared at Grace and walked slowly toward the side of the house.

"We're going to make up a story to tell Chuck," Grace said to Pinky and Beth. "It will be really funny. Can you do it?"

5

ernadette squinted into the sun when she emerged
from Hilda's house fifteen minutes later.

"The visit is over," she announced. "I told Hilda that
we'd be back in a couple of days. The old girl doesn't get
much company."

She walked around the car to the driver's side and
opened the door.

"What are you so happy about?" she said over the top
of the car to Pinky. "Bethie, cat got your tongue, too?"

"Grace told us a funny story," Beth said with a straight
face.

"Must have been a good one." Bernadette wriggled her
shoulders before sliding into her seat. "We had a good old
visit, but I think Hilda has cooties in there. Now it's time
to see if Chuck burned the cabin down."

Pinky and Beth scrambled into the seat behind
Bernadette, leaving the front seat and the station wagon's
third row open. Grace ambled to the back of the car and

turned the door handle. Was this really happening? It wasn't as if Bernadette had twenty kids. She had five. She had brought four of them to Hilda's. Now she was leaving with three.

It *was* funny. The sad thing was that there was no one to share it with. Grace reflected on the injustice of being twinless. Two herselves would appreciate how great she was. As a second choice, Polly could laugh with her, except that Polly was the victim.

"Here we go," Bernadette said as Grace pulled the door shut. "Ready or not."

Would Bernadette blame Grace for forgetting Polly? Did a fog of cigarette smoke, pots of coffee, nightly beer, and excessive naps make you incapable of counting to four? Was Bernadette a mess because she liked those things, or did she like those things because she was a mess? Grace's thoughts shifted to poor Polly. What would she, Grace, do if she were left behind?

"Gracie, do we need anything from the store?" Bernadette called back as they turned onto Main Street.

"Hot dog buns," said Grace as a flat-front building with high windows came into view. It might have been a prison except for the word STORE in red letters. The O was an apple in peeling paint. A hardware store next door provided a bench for a few elderly men in flannel shirts.

"Where are all the kids?" Beth asked, taking in the hardware society.

"Mom, look, ice cream!" Pinky screamed.

"Icey Ices," Bernadette said. "How could I forget?"

Grace turned in her backward-facing seat to look through the front windshield. Just ahead, two poles created a V, arms holding a giant ice-cream cone. The vanilla scoops were weathered down to the metal in patches.

"Please, Mom, can we stop?" Pinky begged.

"You just had lunch."

Pinky didn't answer. He wouldn't say that his lunch was a saltine from the Dark Ages, Grace knew. Bernadette might start railing about lack of appreciation. She might sail right by Icey Ices.

"Oh, I suppose we can get ice cream," Bernadette said, turning sharply into the parking lot. "I'm made out of money, after all. Get out and order. Gracie, here's some cash."

As if they were magnets, Beth and Pinky were pulled to one of the two screened windows. Pinky, a graduate of second grade, read the words out loud with pride.

"Cones," he said solemnly, fixated on the menu nailed between the Order and Pick-up windows. "Vanilla. Chocolate. Strawberry."

Grace heard Chuck's voice in her head. "Bones," he would read for "Cones." "Godzilla. Cheetah. Ratberry." Or something worse. Whoever couldn't read would start to cry. Bernadette would yell at Chuck. That was last summer. He didn't seem to have matured.

"I want vanilla," Beth said to Pinky as if she were telling him a secret.

"There's more stuff on the menu," Pinky said.

"A vanilla cone is the best," said Beth.

Pinky stood in front of the Order window, which reminded Grace of the confessional at church. "I coveted my neighbor's root beer float four times," she imagined saying to the girl behind the screen.

"Two vanilla cones," Pinky said very slowly and clearly.

"Throw a Coke on there," Bernadette said, coming from behind them. "Large. What's the matter with you, Gracie? Nothing for you?"

Grace felt as if someone's fist was in her stomach. Why was she upset? No one else was. The joke on Polly wasn't funny anymore. She could blurt something out and act surprised, as if she had just noticed that her sister was missing.

"Gracie, you don't want anything?" Bernadette asked.

Beth walked up to Bernadette. "Mommy, where is Polly?"

"Polly?" Bernadette did a slow 180-degree turn to scan the street in front of Icey Ices. "Polly, where are you?" she yelled as if Polly had outwitted her by becoming invisible. "Grace, where is your sister?" she demanded, hands on hips.

"I don't know," Grace said, trying to look dumbfounded. "She was playing by herself at Hilda's."

"Get in the car. Everybody. Now!" Bernadette commanded.

Pinky and Beth looked as if they had been told to lie under the wheels.

"My ice cream," Beth sobbed.

"Hold those cones!" Bernadette called to the girl behind the screen. She started the car before anyone was in it. Grace pushed Beth from behind, fearful that Bernadette would drive away with only half of Beth inside. Bernadette had the instinct to find her offspring, even though she would blow smoke all over them once they had been retrieved.

As the car careened around Hilda's corner, Polly came into view. She was sitting on the flat brown grass, her head hanging. Bernadette honked and startled Polly into looking up. Her face was streaked with tears.

"You left me," she said, putting her face down on her arms as the car jerked to a stop in front of her.

"Get in, Pol," said Bernadette.

Polly rose slowly and opened the station wagon's middle door. She didn't seem to notice that she would be squashed in with her siblings. Everyone scooted over as if Polly had something contagious.

"Polly, Polly, Polly," said Bernadette, shaking her head as she pulled away from Hilda's crumbling curb. "You have to pay attention. Bethie is the only one who noticed you were playing hide-and-seek with yourself." She turned the car radio on.

Polly stared at Grace with bewilderment, then put her hand in the book bag she always carried and produced a small jar. She held it low.

"Liniment," she said in an almost inaudible voice. "And I saw Gunda." She turned and looked out the window.

"What was she like?" Grace whispered.

"She scared me."

"Because she was scary or because she did something to scare you?"

"Both. You owe me fifty cents."

"Tell me what happened."

"Not now."

"Later?"

"Okay."

"We're back at the Ices," Beth said in her soft voice. "We're going to start again."

6

W hat's for lunch?" Chuck demanded when everyone had filed back into the cabin.

"You're fifteen years old and you can't get your own lunch?" Bernadette said. "Please, Chuck."

Grace brushed by him. "We not only had lunch, we stopped for ice cream."

"No fair."

"You should have gone with us," said Grace, wondering at his lack of originality. In their family, "no fair" was meaningless.

Bernadette opened the refrigerator and then the little door on the freezer compartment. She banged a couple of ice cubes out of the tray and put them into a jelly glass, filled it with Tahitian Treat, and went to the porch.

"We had fun, didn't we, Polly?" Grace asked as she sat down. Would Polly play?

"Of course we did," Polly said. "How could we not have fun? Hilda had all those candy dishes. It was better than Halloween."

"I thought you had lunch," Chuck said, pulling a chair out for himself at the table.

Grace winked at Beth.

"We had hot dogs for lunch," Beth said. "Fat ones."

"You had hot dogs and candy?" Chuck wailed. "And you didn't bring anything for me?"

Grace could almost taste a juicy hot dog. She couldn't be the only one still hungry after a cracker-and-ice-cream lunch.

"We played games, too," said Pinky.

"What games?"

"What was that game I liked, Grace?" Polly said, flashing distress.

"Bingo. With little pieces of corn that go on the squares."

"Bingo," Pinky repeated.

"That's a stupid game," Chuck said. "It's for old people."

"It's fun when you get prizes," said Polly.

"I don't see any prizes."

"We won candy bars. I ate three. Hilda buys boxes of them," Polly said.

"What about that Grunda person?"

"Gunda," Grace corrected him. "She was interesting."

"Right." Chuck sneered. "She's *Mom's* age. How interesting could she be?"

"She read our palms," said Grace. "She said we have a brother who won't finish high school."

Chuck turned away in disgust. Then he turned back. "Well, maybe I'll go next time. Just so you can't make up any more stuff about what happened."

"I hope we can go back tomorrow," Beth said, the words falling sweetly.

"Me too," Pinky said.

Pinky and Beth fell asleep late in the afternoon. Grace checked on them to make sure they were really out before she went down to the beach with Polly.

"Tell me everything that happened from the second you left us," Grace said to Polly, who drew in the sand with a stick.

"Why should I? You still owe me fifty cents."

"Just tell me, Polly. You know you're going to."

Polly shot Grace a pursed-lip look, then began making deeper lines in the sand. "I went around to the side of the house. A window was open in the back room."

"What about the screen?"

"There wasn't one. That's why I picked it."

"Then what?"

"I had to find an opening between these really heavy

curtains. It was dark in that room. The inside door was shut, but I could hear Mom's voice."

"Then?"

"I felt a dresser top with little jars and bottles on it. So I picked up a couple and smelled them. That's how I found the one I brought outside."

"What about Gunda?"

"I figured she was napping."

"So you got the jar," Grace said. How could she have a sister with more nerve than she had? Especially a younger one. Especially Polly.

"I could tell it was something stinky, so I put it in my pocket. Then I started for the window—just a couple of steps—and something grunted."

"Grunted?"

"It was Gunda. She was trying to talk, but I couldn't understand her. It was just a lot of sounds," Polly said, looking wretched.

Grace took heart. Polly could act brave. But she wasn't brave inside.

"My eyes must have gotten used to the dark," Polly continued. "I didn't want to look, but I couldn't help it. That Gunda, or whatever it was, sat up in bed and saw me. She was kind of like a box with a head on it, and she stared at me as if she couldn't figure out what I was. Then she made that sound again." Polly scrunched her face up in misery. "I was so scared that I got tangled up in the curtains. I had to feel for the opening again. Then I fell through the window. But I got up and ran. When I made it to the street, the car was gone."

The water lapped gently. It didn't seem to be the same water that had taken Beth out so far earlier in the day. Everyone was safe. That made Grace feel generous. She decided to give Polly a break.

"You didn't get caught, Polly," she said. "Think of that."

"That *is* something, isn't it, Grace?" But Polly didn't look relieved.

7

When Grace woke up the next morning, she heard Pinky ask Chuck to take him swimming.

"Can't do it today, Pinky," Chuck said. "Got plans."

From underneath her sheet, Grace directed her voice at Chuck. "Plans to lower your IQ by the hour," she said.

Pinky didn't say anything. Grace imagined his disappointment. Little kids loved big kids, and big kids forgot that little kids existed. She would have to threaten Chuck into doing something with Pinky soon.

"Frankie's dad is taking us into town after they finish cleaning fish they're going to catch this morning. We're going bowling."

"I was in that town, and there's no bowling unless you want to knock over some guys in flannel shirts."

"Not Bagley. Ravensville. The big town."

"As if I care." Not only had Chuck gotten out of going to Hilda's, now he was hanging out with Frankie. Frankie, the only reason to be at this cabin, had not been seen by her for twenty-four hours. Grace opened her eyes and looked at the sunlight through the sheet. Don't give up, she said to herself.

The day seemed to be the longest in Grace's life. Bernadette napped. The little kids made sand castles and swam with their feet touching bottom. Polly read with her feet in the water. Grace stared at the horizon. Chuck came home as Grace began making supper, even though it was only four o'clock. She was opening a can of beans when he barged through the door.

"You wouldn't believe how much fun we had," Chuck said, as if he had forgotten who Grace was and thought she would care about his day. "When I got my third strike, Frankie's dad bought a bag of chips just for me. He said it would slow me down, you know, even out the competition."

Polly slept on the frayed braided rug, a line of drool escaping from her mouth. Pinky and Beth sat across the table from each other, a Chinese checkers game in between them. Pinky was writing the rules on a sheet of paper as they made them up.

"That makes sense," Grace said to Chuck. "If your fingers got any fatter, they wouldn't fit into any bowling ball in the world."

She thought about Frankie as she stirred the canned

baked beans. Why hadn't he asked her to go bowling? He should have. For starters, she could swim faster than Chuck. So it followed that she would be the better bowler, if you considered bowling an athletic skill. Second, she was more entertaining. But Frankie wouldn't know that.

Maybe she wasn't as cute as she needed to be to attract boys. She wasn't Natalie Wood, but she wasn't a cyclops, either. Some people thought her hair was weird. Todd Marconi called her "Catsup and Mustard" before he flunked fifth grade and wasn't in her class anymore.

"May I have supper?" Beth asked.

"Sure. Hot or cold hot dog?"

"What are you going to have?"

"Hot."

"I want mine hot, too. May I have a bun?"

"There aren't any, but there's some bread around here. We'll make a bun."

"Oh, good," Beth said, looking pleased. "We can wrap the hot dogs up."

"Right. Do you want some beans?" Grace asked as she put them on Beth's plate.

"Do we have any grapes?" said Pinky.

Pinky was a hard case. When she was eight, Grace had taken care of Pinky as well as the baby, Beth. Now it was different. Sometimes Pinky got to be a kid. Other times, Grace told him to take care of himself.

"All right, but you get the silverware out for everyone first. It's in the drawer by the sink."

Pinky began rooting around in the drawer while Grace continued dishing up four plates. Bernadette and Chuck could get their own supper.

After the kids had eaten their hot dogs in bread blankets and the beans and grapes, Grace told them to clear the table while she went down to the beach. That would keep them busy for about thirty seconds.

"Hey, Red," called a voice from the Hale property as Grace headed for the wooden steps. Grandpa Ernest Hale waved a neighborly greeting at Grace.

"Hi," she called back, wondering where Frankie Hale was. She ran down the stairs. Stomach on the warm sand, chin on her overlapped hands, she looked over the water. The waves were intoxicating. But the days loomed long and full of family she couldn't shake off. At home she had friends, a phone, a bike that made life bearable. Here she could read, but she couldn't read all day long. She could walk, but without a destination. She could bake, but Chuck would eat most of whatever she made.

Tentative footsteps descended the steps to the beach. Perhaps it was Polly coming to strike a deal? Grace lifted her head and looked at the bare legs on top of the bare feet that weren't her sister's. Cut-offs, T-shirt, a neck with Frankie's head on it.

"Hi," he said. "What are you doing?"

"Nothing," Grace said, because that was the only word she could find in her mouth. A giant hand clutched her throat.

"Me either." Frankie swallowed hard and toed the sand for a minute. "I'm not doing much."

"There's not much going on, I guess."

"I guess not." Frankie paused. "Is Chuck down here?" He looked past Grace at the lake as if expecting to see Chuck waving out there.

"No," Grace squeaked.

"So he's in the cabin?"

"Yes."

"I suppose I can find him there."

"I suppose."

"See you around," Frankie said.

Grace watched Frankie turn back toward the cabin and climb the steps. What had happened? Frankie wanted Chuck for his friend, and she was left with Hilda and Gunda and Bernadette and the kids. Grace put her forehead on the sand.

Footsteps ran down the stairs lightly. Pinky approached Grace's head, which Grace didn't bother to raise.

"What did he want?" he said breathlessly.

"Who?" Grace murmured into the sand.

"Frankie. He came to the door and asked for you, and Polly said you weren't there. Then he came down here. I watched him."

Grace raised herself on one elbow. "Pinky, are you sure he was looking for me?"

"He said, 'Where's your sister?' I don't think he meant Polly because Polly was talking to him." Pinky looked puzzled. "Do you think he meant Bethie?"

Grace rested her head on the sand again, keeping her nose and mouth clear. Frankie had been looking for her. She hadn't understood. She had turned him away. For all her bluster, she, Grace Doyle, knew nothing.

8

The next day, Grace gave up on the idea of ever seeing Frankie again. She pretended that he had left for home with his father and grandfather, which could have happened under other circumstances.

"We're going fishing. See you guys later," Chuck announced, looking smug, after finishing his cereal.

"We're going fishing?" Pinky said, looking up from a comic book.

"No, Frankie and I are going fishing."

"I would like to go, too. Please."

"No, Pinky, Frankie and I are going. We can't watch you and fish at the same time."

Pinky's eyes began to fill, causing the rims to look more pink than usual. He mumbled something to the floor.

"What did you say, Pinky?" Grace asked.

He squeezed his eyelids tightly to hold back the tears, but they leaked out.

"Pinky, what did you say?" Grace repeated. Chuck wasn't going to get off lightly. Let him see Pinky suffer. "Tell me."

"I said," Pinky answered, covering his eyes with his hands, "I said I can watch myself."

The porch door slammed. Frankie stood in the doorway, holding two fishing poles. "Sorry," he said. "Should I come back later?"

Grace looked at him. He was already gone, as far as she was concerned. She could say whatever she wanted. "Chuck won't let Pinky go fishing with you guys," she said. "And that stinks."

"He can come with us," Frankie said. "Come on, Pinky. You can pick out a pole. Let's go. We're getting a late start."

Pinky followed Frankie through the porch and out the door, blinking hard. Chuck glared at Grace as he walked by her. She glared back.

"Hey, Grace," Frankie called back into the house. "Let's go swimming when I get back this afternoon."

"Sure," Grace called before she knew it was her voice that had answered. It was so easy. He had asked. She had responded. Words, but no face-to-face. How simple was that?

"Grace," Polly said from a chair in the corner of the room, where she had been reading. "Frankie is really cute, isn't he?"

"He's nice," said Beth, who had resumed drawing at the table.

"He's okay," Grace said.

Chuck, Grace, Polly, Pinky, Beth, and Frankie spent the afternoon on the beach. Grace and Frankie swam, Chuck floated in the inner tube, and Polly lounged at the edge of the water with Pinky and Beth, who mimicked swimming by walking on their hands while splashing with their feet. Grace told the two little ones when it was time for a shade break.

"May we come out now, Gracie?" Beth asked when the swimmers returned.

"In a little while," Grace said. She had ordered them under their beach towels. "You don't want to turn into lobsters. Do you need some more comics?"

Later Frankie sat next to Grace when they played old maid with everyone except for Chuck, who disliked card games. "I have to go with my dad and grandpa to visit my grandpa's brother tomorrow. He's an invalid."

"Then I guess you'll be here on Friday," Grace said.

"Right. We'll be here for the weekend."

"So will we."

"And next week."

"For most of it."

"Maybe we can spend every day together," said Polly, whose shoulders were very pink.

"Here's your T-shirt, Pol," Grace said, swiveling to pick it out of the sand behind her. "You're getting burned."

"I'm going fishing with Chuck in the morning on Friday," Frankie said. "And Pinky. I'll see you after that, Grace."

"I love fishing," said Pinky, who had returned from his expedition with two sunfish that were swimming in a bucket in front of the porch.

"I love the cabin," Beth said.

Frankie and Grace looked at each other and smiled.

How had so much changed so quickly? Grace wished that she could stretch the day like a rubber band into twice its length.

"Let's eat supper on the beach," she said.

"But first we'll finish this game," said Beth.

"Sure, Bethie. Then we'll put the sun to bed."

9

Grace survived Thursday, the day that Frankie was gone, by reliving the previous day. As she made fudge in the morning and sand castles in the afternoon with Pinky and Beth and Polly, she thought about how Frankie had stayed by her on the beach. She never had time to wonder where he was. He was always there. She was there for him, too, quipping, laughing, reaching for the catsup bottle at the same second.

On Friday morning, Bernadette announced another Hilda and Gunda expedition.

"Your father is coming up tomorrow, and he sure as heck won't want to play Little Red Riding Hood," she said to Grace. "No visiting any grannies while he's here."

"I promised Beth that we would make scrapbooks this morning," Grace said, hoping that she would be rescued from this craft ordeal when Frankie returned.

"That should take about ten minutes," said Bernadette.

"It's a very big project. Besides, it's Chuck's turn to go. All he does is sit around and eat. Take him."

"I suppose I could," Bernadette said. "At least I wouldn't break the bank at Icey Ices if I only take one kid with me."

Too nervous to feel victorious, Grace kept her lips together.

Through the windows, the sky shone intensely, promisingly blue.

Polly walked into the main room with a threadbare beach towel. "Hi, Grace," she said on her way to the door.

"Hi, Pol." She felt sorry for Polly because Polly would never be her. "Don't forget we're going to make scrapbooks later."

On his way into the cabin, Chuck almost collided with Polly. "Forgot my pail," he said. "I'm going fishing."

"Sorry, Chuck, we're going to see Hilda this morning," Bernadette said, pausing for a sip of steaming coffee. "Might as well leave before it gets any hotter."

"Ma, it's hot already. Besides, I made plans with Frankie."

Happiness rose in Grace like the mercury in a thermometer. Maybe he wasn't going fishing with Frankie after all.

"No lip, Chuck," said Bernadette. "You have to put your time in like the others did."

"Can I drive?" Chuck begged. "Please, can I at least drive?"

"Aren't you the kid who hasn't studied for his permit test? No permit, no driving." Bernadette lit her cigarette and waved the match in the air. "I value my life. Now I need to finish working on my hair."

"Say hi to Gunda for me," Grace said.

Chuck walked to the box of old comics he had brought from home and grabbed a stack. "This is all your fault," he said to Grace as he passed by her. "I could have been fishing."

"Hey, Chuck," Frankie called through the screen door. "Are you ready?"

"Oh, man, I gotta visit some ancient people with my mom," Chuck moaned as he opened the door. Frankie stepped into the porch and waved at Grace.

"That's too bad," he said. "We can fish tomorrow morning. Or the next day."

Frankie noticed Pinky staring at him. "You too," he said. Pinky relaxed.

"Wait a minute, Frankie," Chuck said. "You can come with me, now."

Bernadette emerged from the hallway with a can of hair spray. She lipped her cigarette as she gave herself a final misting, setting the can down on the table when she had finished.

"Jeez, Ma, you're killing me," Chuck said, coughing.

"Let's get going, then."

"Can Frankie come with us?"

"I guess so, if you two don't ask for anything or run away like Polly did."

Everything was wrong. The joke had turned into an excursion for Chuck and Frankie.

"Polly ran away from what?" Chuck said to Grace.

"Polly didn't run away. She was playing outside and we forgot her." She turned to Bernadette, who was trying to stuff a can of Tahitian Treat into the pocket of her pedal pushers. It wouldn't go. "Bernadette, maybe Chuck should stay here and help with the kids."

"Too late, Gracie. We're gone. You need Chuck like you need a hole in the head."

"I have to get some money from my dad," Frankie said as he headed for the door. "There's a place to buy ice cream in that little town."

"Will we make scrapbooks now, Gracie?" Beth asked from her chair by the window. "You told Mommy that we're going to make scrapbooks."

"Have fun, kids," Chuck drawled. "Have fun with your arts and crafts teacher."

"C'mon, Chuck, I don't have all day," Bernadette called from the porch. "Here comes your friend."

Grace heard three car doors slam, one after the other. She walked to the porch and watched the car back away from the cabin.

10

"Is it time to make the scrapbooks now?" Beth called to Grace, who was on the porch setting up a card table. At least they might catch a breeze.

"Sure. But first we have to find something to use for pages. Your tablet is too small. There has to be some blank paper around here somewhere. You and Pinky search the big room."

Rummaging through a cupboard on the porch, Grace found a lot of mouse turds. Maybe the bedrooms would be more fruitful. As Grace headed to the hallway, Pinky triumphantly held up a thin piece of cardboard.

"Good job, Pinky," Grace said. "Now see if you can find a few more."

In Bernadette's bedroom, an old-fashioned chiffonier yielded dresses and hats that must have been Aunt Marie's. Grace reconsidered the scrapbook plan. They could play dress-up instead. Would that be easier?

Curious about anything out of sight, Grace pulled a

chair to a tall, narrow chest of drawers. She stepped onto the chair and then up onto her toes to begin at the top. Two photo albums covered with dust crowned the chest. Pull out the pictures and two empty scrapbooks awaited. Maybe Polly could find her own pages.

"What did you find, Gracie?" asked Beth, standing at Grace's feet.

"Scrapbooks for you and Pinky. We should wipe them off." She held the albums to her chest and jumped down from the chair. Surveying the floor, she spied one of Bernadette's bobby sox. She picked it up and dusted the albums.

"Here you go, Bethie. Let's bring Pinky's to him."

"Then what will we do?"

"First, take the old pictures out. Then put in anything you want—pictures from magazines, pictures you drew in your tablet, flowers, anything."

"Money?"

Where did Beth get her ideas? Would her goofy little brain work in the world?

"You can put a penny in if you want. But if you keep the penny, you can buy something."

"A penny," said Beth dreamily. "I have a penny with my birthday on it."

"Your birth year, Bethie. Money doesn't have actual birth dates on it. Let's take these scrapbooks to the porch."

"Where's my album?" said Polly, who had just returned from the beach as dry as when she had left, Grace noted. Morning, too cool. She had been there.

"Use Pinky's cardboard and some tablet paper taped together or something. Polly, you have to try harder to find your own."

Polly sat next to Beth, who began to gently remove the black-and-white photos from their triangular corners.

"Do you think we should be messing with these?" Polly said to Grace.

"Nobody cares about these old pictures. They were rotting away up there," Grace said, although she had wondered the same thing when Pinky had begun ripping the photos out of his album.

"Mom might want them," Polly said.

"She doesn't know they're here," said Grace, her guilt growing along with the piles of snapshots.

"I know what we can do," suggested Pinky, as he continued to yank out pictures. "We can put them back where you found the albums."

"Now, that's using your noggin," Grace said. Why hadn't she thought of that?

"What's the matter with this little girl?" Beth asked, looking at a photo she had removed.

"Who?" asked Grace.

Polly stared at the picture. Pinky stood up and peered over Polly's shoulder.

"Let me see it closer," said Grace. Beth released her hold.

Two women smiled in the photo. Their short hair was almost hidden under the brims of straw hats, and they wore short-sleeved dresses with slightly dropped waists and skirts that showed a bit of ankle. One woman held a baby, its face turned from the camera. In front of the other woman stood a little girl, eight or nine years old.

Beth knelt on the chair in order to see the snapshot better. "What's the matter with the girl holding the doll?" she said.

The girl stared out of the photo with a lifeless expression. Grace stared back. The girl wasn't holding the baby doll in front of her. Her arms hung at her sides. The woman behind the little girl was holding the doll in place.

Polly swallowed hard. "I think it's her."

"Who?" Grace said.

"That Gunda woman. No expression."

If that was Gunda, Grace thought, the woman holding the doll might be her mother, Hilda. Hilda didn't look crooked. She looked straight and happy in spite of having to hold Gunda's doll for her. The other woman might be one of Hilda's sisters, Grandma or Aunt Marie.

"The baby," Polly said. "That baby could be Mom."

"What is wrong with the little girl?" Beth asked again.

"The little girl's brain wasn't right," Grace said. "I think she was born with only part of a brain or something."

"Let me see," said Pinky, struggling to get a look. "Oh, I thought maybe her head would be smaller." He settled back in his seat and continued piling up photos.

"That look," Polly said. "That's her look."

The women seemed so lighthearted to Grace. Would they have been as happy if they knew the little girl would grow up and scare kids? Would they have been thrilled to know that the baby would grow up to be Bernadette? What about Hilda? What if she had known that she would turn into a human pretzel?

Grace stared at the faces, then turned her attention to the background. They stood in front of a house with a porch. It looked different in black-and-white, but she was certain. They were at the cabin that Grandpa Olav had built for his wife and three daughters.

"Let's get going," Grace said. "I'll read to you while you work." She picked a *Reader's Digest* from a stack of magazines, stuck the photo inside, and began reading from "Laughter Is the Best Medicine." Grace didn't want to think about the picture. Those people couldn't see their fates. They would turn into a grownup Gunda, a grownup Bernadette, and a Hilda, grown facedown. Or, in the case of Grandma or Aunt Marie, dead.

A car honked outside the cabin.

"Polly, why don't you go see who that is?" Grace said.

"It sounds like Mom's car."

"She couldn't be back this early. Go and see."

"Grace, why me? Why can't you go?"

"I'm trying to help you become a responsible person."

"Keep reading, Grace," Pinky said. "This is so funny."

"Polly will read. I'll go, I'll go," Grace said, thrusting the magazine at Polly. Reading out loud to the kids reminded her that she wasn't reading what she wanted to read to herself. "I'll go this time."

Polly was right. Bernadette sat behind the wheel of the station wagon. Hilda sat next to her, low in the passenger seat.

"We were just staring at Hilda's walls, so I thought I'd take her out on a Sunday drive even though it isn't Sunday," Bernadette said. "Gracie, run and get the pack of cigarettes on the dresser as long as you're out here."

"Hello, Grace," Hilda said with a little wave. "It's lovely to see you again. This is my Gunda in the back."

Grace stopped breathing. She hadn't looked beyond Bernadette and Hilda.

Hilda made an attempt to look behind her, but she was too low to see over the top of the seat. Grace's eyes went from Hilda's sweet smile to the backseat, where Gunda sat stiffly, staring at Grace. In her plaid summer dress, Gunda looked as startled as Grace felt. "Ma," Gunda uttered, the syllable laced with concern. She moved her hand over the seat to the top of Hilda's head.

Hilda raised her hand and gently patted Gunda's larger one. "You're all right, dear," she said. "This nice girl is

Grace, Bernadette's daughter. Don't you worry, we're going home now."

"Enough of a field trip for one day," Bernadette said. Grace realized that the car was still running. "You can see the rest of the gang another time, Gun. Grace, go grab those cigarettes."

"Thank you for coming out to see us, Grace," called Hilda in her fragile voice as Grace sprinted into the cabin.

"Who was out there?" Polly asked.

"Bernadette forgot her cigs," said Grace. She understood why Polly hadn't wanted to discuss Gunda. She didn't either. The sight of a grownup body without much of a thinking part was enough to shock anyone except Bernadette into silence.

11

Early in the afternoon, Bernadette clattered onto the porch alone.

"Everybody survived?" she asked Grace.

"Still four of us here, last time I counted."

"Great, I can steal a little shut-eye." She surveyed the card table top covered with elbows, magazines, and the remnants of lunch. "Hey, kids," she said. In the big room, she paused at the refrigerator for a can of pop. "Don't wake me up if anyone needs me. I have to get my beauty sleep before your dad shows up tomorrow."

Voices slipped in from outside.

"I'll be back," said Grace, pushing herself up from the chair. Beth didn't seem to notice that Grace was leaving. She was intent on pasting an acorn onto an album page. It rolled off when she pressed it. Grace paused. "Bethie, I don't think that's going to work."

Having finished his scrapbook, Pinky looked up from one of Chuck's comic books to watch Beth. "It might work," he said. "Put some more paste on, but don't push down. Let it sit and dry."

Polly stopped cutting the old curtains she had found in a drawer. She was using her tablet-paper scrapbook for clothing design.

"She won't be able to close it," she said to Pinky.

"Maybe she doesn't want to close it," he said, observing the acorn attempt.

"Yes, it will be a pretty book that stays open," Beth said, licking paste off her finger.

Grace walked slowly to the door. Sometimes the sweetness of the little kids was upsetting. Would Pinky ever be tough enough to weather the challenges of growing up? Would Beth? It was doubtful.

The voices had moved down the steps to the beach. Grace followed. Frankie and Chuck were sitting on the sand.

"How was Hilda?" she said. "And Gunda?" For the first time, she realized that she hadn't thought about Chuck and Frankie's whereabouts during Bernadette's Sunday drive.

"We didn't go see them," said Chuck.

"Impossible. You left with Bernadette."

"No, really," Frankie said. "Your brother complained so much that your mom dropped us off at the dock in town before she went to see those people. We had our poles when we hopped into the car, so we fished the whole time."

Grace looked at Chuck to see if they were lying. He pointed to a bucket. Fish swam merrily or frantically, depending on whether you were the cook or the fish.

"Dinner," Chuck said. He glowed.

"Who's going to clean them, your servant?" Grace bit her tongue. She should watch her tone in front of Frankie.

"I know how to clean them," Frankie said. "I've been cleaning fish with my grandpa since he let me hold a knife."

"You didn't even stop at Hilda's?" Grace said. "You just fished?"

"We went to Icey Ices," said Chuck. "It wasn't that far from the dock. Then we fished some more."

Grace felt the day slipping away from her. If Frankie wasn't going to act, she would. "Who gets all those fish?" she asked. "Let's eat them together, since you both caught them."

"That's a good idea," Frankie said. "My dad and grandpa might like that."

"But with my mom?" said Chuck. "And the kids?"

"It's a good plan," Grace said. "I'll tell Bernadette when she gets up."

They ate supper at a long table on the Hales' porch. Frankie's dad and grandpa sat at one end. Grace was at the other end, as far away from Bernadette as possible. Frankie sat next to Grace, and Chuck next to Frankie. Pinky and Beth clustered in the middle with Polly.

"These fish are great," Bernadette said, licking her fingers. She wore a white peasant blouse that left her shoulders almost bare. Her lipstick matched the red trim of her top. Dark curls sprang from her headband. Grace was grateful that she had Dad's reddish hair so that hers didn't totally mimic Bernadette's.

"How is it that you haven't been up here for so many years, Bernie?" asked Grandpa Ernest. "I haven't seen you since you were very young, a teenager."

In spite of herself, Grace watched Bernadette, trying to imagine how other people saw her. Frankie was watching her, too.

"You knew the three sisters," Bernadette said. "Hilda avoided the cabin after Gunda's accident. Mom—one of the sisters—and Dad brought me up here when I was a kid. But when Aunt Marie retired, she lived at the cabin in the summer. She wasn't too crazy about kids, so we didn't come to visit often. My husband and I brought Chuck and Grace here when they were little, but the circus was a bit much for Marie." Bernadette speared a piece of the fried fish and resumed eating.

"Marie kept to herself, but she was a gracious woman," said Grandpa Ernest. "Hilda, however, was the one I set my sights on when I was young."

"Wasn't she too old for you?" Grace said from the other end of the table.

"Where do you get your manners, Gracie?" said Bernadette, after having made a show of choking on her fish.

"Hilda, your great-aunt, is two or three years older than I am," Grandpa Ernest said with a smile. "We spent summers next door to each other. From the moment I was aware of her existence in the world, Hilda was the one for me. As much as a ten-year-old can love a thirteen-year-old, or a fifteen-year-old can love an eighteen-year-old, that's how smitten I was with Hilda. She and Harold had their wedding reception at the cabin. I hid in the woods."

"She broke your heart," Beth said.

Grandpa Ernest looked at Beth. "She did, but she never knew it." He took a sip of the iced tea that Grace had made. "So I found another girl, my Julie."

"That's good," said Beth, nibbling a potato chip Bernadette had contributed to the supper.

"Hilda's still real nice," Bernadette interjected. "But she's not what you'd call a looker anymore."

"And your cousin, Gunda?" asked Frankie's dad.

"I drove her and Hilda out here on a little jaunt today."

"And I missed her?" Grandpa Ernest said loudly.

"We were just here for a second. I could have brought them over, Ernest, but I didn't think of it. Sorry."

Grace looked at Polly, who was frowning at her plate as if she could see Gunda's large shadowy figure.

Pinky's eyes darted from face to face as if everyone knew something that he didn't.

"What's wrong with Gunda's brain again?" he asked.

"She's not right in the head," said Grace. "Bernadette told us."

"Why isn't she right in the head?" Pinky restated his question. No one said anything. Wasn't Bernadette supposed to answer?

Grandpa Ernest cleared his throat. He looked at Bernadette. She looked back at him as if she expected him to speak.

"As I recall, Gunda fell in the lake when she was a toddler. Is that correct, Bernie?"

"You're right, Ernest."

"Well, as you know, she lived, but she was in a coma for quite a while. She wasn't the same little girl after that."

Everyone was quiet.

"This lake?" Frankie finally asked.

"Yes," said Grandpa Ernest.

"Where was the little girl's mommy?" Beth said, looking alarmed.

Another silence filled the room.

"I believe that Hilda and Harold had driven into town. Am I right, Bernadette?"

"Right you are," Bernadette answered curtly, then paused. "It's not a happy story, Ernest. Let's have another beer."

Grandpa Ernest is trying to get Bernadette to run with this, Grace realized.

"Marie was watching Gunda at the time, I believe," Grandpa said.

"Right again. Marie was the youngest sister. She was crazy about Gunda."

Grandpa waited for Bernadette to speak again.

"Marie turned her back on Gunda for a minute. A minute too long." Bernadette looked uncomfortable.

"Hilda and Harold rarely, if ever, came back to the cabin after that," said Grandpa. "Hilda, as you know, wanted nothing to do with the cabin after Marie died. Do you want to tell the rest, Bernie?"

"You're doing great, Ernest."

Grandpa scanned the faces at the table. "Your great-aunt Marie broke her engagement to her fiancé soon after Gunda's accident. After that, she worked as a secretary at the mill in town and lived with her parents."

"Why didn't she get married?" said Polly.

Grandpa cleared his throat. "I imagine that she felt, somehow, unworthy."

"Why did she come back to the lake in the summer after she retired?" Grace asked. "After all those years?"

"I've often wondered the same thing," Grandpa said. "Perhaps it was her penance."

"What is 'her penance'?" said Beth.

"A punishment," Grandpa said, looking at her with

concern. "She never forgave herself for what happened to little Gunda. I think she punished herself over and over."

"Oh," Beth said. "She could have been the little girl's good auntie."

"All right, that's enough," Bernadette said. "Marie never got over it. God knows Hilda didn't have a choice. She couldn't go into her shell with Gunda to look after. End of story. Any more beer here?"

"Where is the little girl now?" Beth asked.

Everyone looked at Beth as if aliens had just discarded her.

"That's Gunda," Grace said. "She's old, older than Bernadette."

"I'm sad for her. She couldn't hold her doll by herself."

Bernadette frowned at Beth and opened the bottle of Hamm's that Frankie's dad had put in front of her.

"The things that you think up, Bethie," said Bernadette. She adjusted her peasant blouse, covering her shoulders as if suddenly realizing that they were cold as well as naked. "Kids. Where do they get these ideas?"

12

After everyone had finished eating, Frankie turned to Grace. "Let's go down to the beach." His brown eyes danced with light, probably reflected from the lantern someone had hung in a corner of the porch to lure bugs away from food and people.

"Yeah, we can look for crawlers in the dirt before we hit the sand," said Chuck, pushing himself away from the table. Polly and Pinky followed suit.

"Grace, you and Polly stay and help me clear the mess we made," Bernadette said.

Grace looked at Frankie, whose eyebrows went up in an I-don't-know-how-this-happened look.

"Let them all go, Bernadette," said Frankie's dad. "We don't have anything else to do except play a little poker."

"I can clear the table," Grace said. What was the point of going to the beach with Frankie when she would be responsible for the younger ones?

"Let's move inside to where the comfortable furniture is," said Tom Hale. "Need another beer, Bernadette?"

"Why not?"

Grace and Grandpa Ernest carried the dishes to the sink.

Every once in a while Bernadette said something beyond unfair to cruel. While Bernadette was at the hospital having Beth, Grace and Dad and Polly had decorated the Christmas tree. Mrs. Anderson from next door brought a Dutch oven of beef stew to Bernadette after the homecoming.

"I can't believe it," Mrs. Anderson had said. "A new baby, and the tree is already decorated."

"You do what you have to do," Bernadette had replied.

"I'll wash if you dry," said Grandpa, snapping Grace back to the present.

"I can help," Frankie's dad said as he shut the refrigerator door with his elbow, a beer in each hand.

"Just take the garbage out, Tom. The fish was great, but I'd rather not smell it in my dreams."

"Sure you don't want to join the kids, Grace?" Tom Hale asked.

"It's early. I will when I'm finished here." Grace looked at Bernadette, who shuffled a deck of cards after tipping her head back for a long swig of her beer. "Lord knows Bernadette won't help. It would cut into her free time. She needs at least twenty-four hours of it a day."

Bernadette put down her bottle.

"Gracie, I swear I don't know where you get that mouth."

"Where do I get that mouth?" Grace echoed. She stared at Bernadette as she dried a glass and placed it in the cupboard. She stopped short of saying, "Look in the mirror," but held herself so that she wouldn't display the tiniest bit of emotion.

Grandpa kept washing dishes. Frankie's dad took a sip of beer and put the bottle down on the table. He suddenly remembered the garbage and jumped up to carry it outside.

"Jeez," Bernadette said to Grace over the sound of running water at the sink. "I'm glad your dad's coming tomorrow. He'll have something to say about your attitude." She resumed her card shuffling.

On the beach, Beth patted sand onto Pinky's stomach, which she tried to bury along with his extremities. Polly sat close to—but not next to—Frankie and Chuck. They stopped their rock-skipping competition when Grace descended the steps.

Frankie smiled. "Hi, Grace."

"Hi."

Chuck looked at Frankie as if he had violated a code. "We're having fun," he said to Grace.

"What should we do, Grace?" Polly asked. "We want to do something."

"We're having fun," Chuck repeated.

"I heard you," Grace said. "Let's play hide-and-seek. The dock is safe."

"Do I have to play?" Pinky asked. "It's cool in here."

Beth continued patting Pinky's neck. "May I play?"

"You don't have to play, Pinky," Grace said. "You can be safe instead of the dock. Beth, you can play, but stay with Polly so you don't get lost."

Polly looked at Grace with quiet desperation. Polly doesn't want to be in charge of Beth, Grace realized. She wants to be free to chase Frankie.

"Polly, this is just the first game. You hide with Beth. Chuck, start counting."

The beach offered no cover. Grace, Frankie, Polly, and Beth scrambled up the steps and into the trees as fast as they could.

"Thirteen, fourteen, fifteen . . . how high, Grace? Fifty?"

"A hundred," she called back. The branches rustled and snapped as everyone scattered. Chuck's counting was punctuated with the soft lapping of the lake. No use going too far. Reaching Pinky would be easy if she ran down the wooded hill rather than the steep steps, where Chuck would most likely be waiting for them. The counting ended. How easy it would be to slide by Chuck.

Grace looked at the sky. It was still blue and a little

hazy. The sun wouldn't go down until almost nine o'clock. She moved through the woods that fronted the cabins until she had a clear view of the beach. Troll-like, Chuck hid under the steps that ended in sand. From the opposite side, Polly and Beth ran, skimming over the ground to Pinky, the human sandbag. By the time Chuck saw them, it was too late.

"Free!" Polly screamed as she and Beth fell on Pinky.

"No fair!" Chuck cried.

"Why not?" Polly shouted. "We have to come back on your route?"

The ground crunched behind Grace. She turned.

"Still hiding?" Frankie said.

Grace swallowed hard. She had never been this close to him. She was tall for a girl, but he was taller. One of his sun-browned arms held a branch out of his face.

"Still hiding," she said. "And you're still hiding?"

"Still hiding."

"We could each run at Pinky from a different side of the beach at the same time," said Grace. "Chuck wouldn't know which one of us to go after."

"That's a good idea."

"I'll go from the left side and you go from the right."

"Okay."

"Let's start now. We're the last ones."

"Okay."

"See you on the beach." Grace began to move away.

"Grace, don't go yet."

"Why not?"

"I want to ask you if you'll go out with me sometime." Frankie sounded out of breath, as if he wasn't used to talking to a girl's face so close.

"I will." Grace found ordinary words for an extraordinary feeling.

"We could walk into town or something."

"Sure. Do you know how far that is?" Grace wanted to take back her question. Maybe Frankie wouldn't want to walk into town if he thought it was an all-day expedition.

"It's about five miles. I watched the odometer when Grandpa drove in the last time."

"That's not too bad," Grace said, feeling hopeful.

"Do you want to go tomorrow?"

"Frankie! Grace! Where are you guys?" Chuck's voice boomed from the lower part of the woods just above the beach. Did he think he could scare them out?

"Tomorrow is good," Grace said, knowing that it wasn't. Tomorrow Dad would arrive. He would notice if she was gone for most of the day.

"Let's leave at about ten o'clock," said Frankie. "There's a little park in town. We can eat lunch there or something."

"Sure. I know there's a grocery store."

They moved in opposite directions. Grace padded through the woods toward the beach, her heart thudding.

What if she was wrong about Frankie and he turned out to be Chuck-like? How could she lose him on a ten-mile hike? Would Bernadette make a fuss if she found out? Grace had never gone on a walk that might or might not be a date.

When Grace and Frankie broke out of the woods and raced for the human sandbag, Chuck was ambling toward Pinky, too. He looked in both directions and made his choice. He went for Grace. She could have guessed it. Chuck would let Frankie beat him rather than see Grace gloat, home free.

When Frankie called "Free!" getting away didn't seem as important. Grace taunted Chuck, forcing him to switch back and forth as she zigzagged in the sand. Game over. She didn't need to win at everything. But Chuck slipped. Grace made a wide arc around him and dove for Pinky.

"I almost had her!" Chuck yelled. "It's like you two planned it."

Grace didn't look at Frankie. "Stuff like this just happens," she said. "It's fun when it does, right, Bethie?"

Beth sat on a rock, smiling her sweet, slightly crazy smile. "It's fun," she said.

13

At a few minutes before ten o'clock in the morning, Grace stuck her head into Bernadette's bedroom. Propped up on pillows, Bernadette was sipping coffee and paging through a magazine.

"I'm going out for a while," said Grace.

"Where, Gracie? There's no place to go around here."

"I'm going on a walk for a couple of hours."

"Man alive. Your father will be here by lunchtime. How am I going to have everything ready if you're off traipsing in the woods?"

Bernadette's larger window faced east. The sun was climbing toward its noontime destination, spreading heat as it rose.

"I'm going crazy being here alone every day," Grace said.

"So take a little walk and be back before lunch."

"I'm walking to town."

"Town? Don't be crazy, Gracie. You won't be back until tonight. You're not going. Case closed." Bernadette straightened the magazine in her lap.

Grace fumed. Was she Bernadette's servant? Nobody paid her to keep everything together.

"I'm leaving. I'll be back when I'm back."

"You're my right-hand man," Bernadette said. "Can't go."

For the most part, Grace did what was expected of her. Give Beth a bath. Iron Dad's shirts. Open chicken noodle soup for supper when Dad worked late. That was her part of the pact. For the most part, Bernadette stayed out of her hair. Why was Bernadette policing her now?

What would Frankie do if she was late? Knock on the door? Or would he leave if she didn't show up outside?

"Gotta go," Grace said. "Train another kid while I'm gone."

"Gracie, you're asking for it."

If Bernadette lurched out of bed, she would spill her coffee and tip the ashtray. She wouldn't get up. Getting up was not convenient.

"See you later," Grace said in a bright voice, as if nothing unpleasant were happening.

"Jeez," Bernadette said behind her.

Polly sat at the table, the only sibling in the room. She paged through a bird book. "What's up today, Grace?" she said.

"I'm going on a hike."

"Can I come?"

"Let me finish. I'm going on a hike. Dad will be here soon."

"When are you coming back?"

"Late. I'm walking into town."

"By yourself?"

For a second, Grace considered telling her. Poor Polly. If there was one thing worse than being Bernadette's oldest daughter, it was being the second daughter. Grace pictured herself as the head housekeeper with the all-important ring of keys at her waist. Polly was the scullery maid. The scullery maid was off dreaming about Frankie, too.

"By myself."

"Please, can I come?"

"Another time."

Frankie stood in the trees between the two cabins with his back to Grace, hands in the pockets of his shorts.

Grace walked slowly and watched the sun sneak through the branches to bathe Frankie's head in stripes of sunlight. He heard her and turned, smiling. She was grateful that she had brushed her teeth and whisked the toast crumbs from the front of her blouse.

Frankie pulled one hand out of his pocket. He held it in front of Grace, his fingers loosely curved into a vase. A

tiny yellow flower peeked out, looking fresh for having
been in a pocket.

"For me?"

Frankie lifted his eyebrows as if to say, Who else?

"Pretty," said Grace, plucking it out of Frankie's
hand-vase. Where could she keep it without carrying it,
purse-like, for five miles and back? Grace put it behind
her ear.

As she lowered her hand, Frankie took it in his. But
somehow he had the wrong hand. Grace and Frankie
faced each other as if they had just shaken hands and not
let go.

"Nice to meet you," Grace said, moving her hand up
and down with Frankie's attached.

"Oops." Frankie let go of Grace's right hand and took
her left. "Let's go to town."

Frankie seemed happy to be in possession of Grace's
hand. But five miles could be a very long walk if no one
spoke.

"Do you have any brothers or sisters?" she asked, after
they turned onto the gravel road from the driveway.

"I have a little brother, Tommy. He's eight. He's with
my mom at her parents'. Sometimes we split up like that.
Last year I went to Chicago with my mom for a weekend.
We'll all be at the lake together in August."

"Aren't there any in-between kids?"

"That's it."

"I'm trying to imagine my family with only Beth and me in it."

"My family seems okay to me. My little brother is a nice guy."

They walked. The sun felt friendly, as if it was painting them evenly with a coat of comfort. Sumac rushed the season with a red leaf drawing attention here and there. A caterpillar neared the end of its desert road, having almost completed its trek to the other side. In the distance, a speck of car grew larger, dust creating a puffy tail behind it.

"Hardly anyone drives this road during the week," Frankie said. "But this is Saturday, isn't it?"

"Days don't matter as much when there's no school."

"What are you good in?" Frankie asked. "At school."

"I like science. There's a lot to think about."

"Reading?"

"I read all the time. Reading is like water. I need it. Do you?"

Before he could answer, Frankie moved with Grace to the side of the road as the oncoming car approached. The driver made a wide arc to avoid them, braked, and then went into reverse. A lost tourist? A car seemed out of place here, where the loudest noises were cicadas and invisible scurrying creatures and snapping twigs.

A man leaned across the front seat and spoke through the passenger window. "Who's that you're attached to, Grace?"

race peered into the car. "Dad, whose wreck is this?"

"Uncle Joe's. I had to figure something out, since your mother stole the wagon."

"I didn't know he had a car that looked this bad."

"Who are you eloping with, Grace?"

Grace leaned on the car's window frame with both elbows. "This is Frankie. He lives next door to the cabin." Dad seemed out of place here. Or maybe it was Frankie.

"How do you do?" Dad said, extending his arm to shake hands with Frankie through the passenger window, as Grace moved out of the way.

"Hello, sir," said Frankie.

Dad's hand slipped back into the car, which stopped rumbling when he turned off the ignition. He opened his door and walked around the front of the car to the other side.

"How are things going, Grace?" he asked.

"The usual."

Frankie was almost as tall as Dad, Grace observed. But Dad was solid, with broad shoulders and a chest designed to repel an attack.

"You two look alike," Frankie said, his eyes moving from Grace to her father.

"It's the hair," Dad said, running a hand through a reddish thatch that was a few shades deeper than Grace's. "And the determined jaw. But you do like her face, even though it resembles mine?"

"Oh, sure, I like it," said Frankie, looking trapped.

"What should I know about the cabin, Grace?" Dad said.

"Bernadette dragged us to see Hilda a few days ago. Polly saw crazy Gunda and acts as if that zapped her brain. Otherwise, things are pretty normal. We could use some more food. We ate at Frankie's grandpa's cabin last night."

"I shopped on the way up. No one should starve for a while. I'd better get going. Nice to meet you, Frankie. By the way, where are you two off to?"

"Town," said Grace.

"So," Dad said, looking at his watch for a few seconds, "with a break for ice cream, you'll be back by two o'clock, maybe two-thirty." He winked at Grace as he lowered himself into the driver's seat. "I never forget a face," he said to Frankie.

"Bye, Dad."

"Bye, Mr. Doyle."

The car started up and diminished in size as it moved away.

"Is your dad strict?" Frankie asked. "I couldn't tell if he was serious or not."

"Serious, not mean." Grace didn't mention that Dad had never said anything about boys and remembering their faces before, probably because she had never been with one.

Five miles was an easy walk. The talking was easy, too. Frankie listened, talked, listened, talked, almost the way Grace's friend Margaret did. This was the opposite of Chuck, whose main topic was himself.

"During the school year, I walked at least two miles a day—to school, home for lunch, back to school, and home again," Grace said. "Next year I'll walk twice as far to high school, but I won't go home for lunch."

The gravel road looked baked, as if pleading for rain to cool it off. Grace didn't mind the heat, although the breeze was welcome.

"Five miles shouldn't be hard for us," said Frankie. "Our legs are kind of like our personal vehicles. One time, for math, we had to think of a problem. Mine was about mileage. If I walked my dog for one mile, how much farther would that be for her based on the length of her legs compared to mine?"

Grace thought for a minute. "You'd both cover the

same number of miles. Her leg length doesn't make any difference."

"Right. Hardly anyone got that. The only difference would depend on who walked on the inside and who walked on the outside of the curve."

"So I'm better at math than most of your classmates."

"Right again."

Frankie understands conversation, Grace thought with gratitude.

"Grandpa told me that your mom shops at the same grocery store as my mom," said Frankie.

"In Bagley?"

"No, at home."

Grace thought that her heart had stopped beating. "Are you sure?"

"That's what Grandpa said."

"That means that we don't live that far apart."

"Four miles, we figured." Frankie squeezed Grace's hand.

"This walk feels as if we're moving on a map," she said because the current topic was too blissfully overwhelming. "I've never walked into a town before in my life."

"It's pretty cool. We're crossing a border. Stepping into new territory. Stuff like that. Let's find someplace to get a drink."

A DINER sign loomed ahead on the edge of town. But

Grace and Frankie decided to stop at a gas station with a pop machine in front. Frankie had change. He put a dime in for Grace, who pushed the Orange Crush button. The bottle hit the bottom with a thunk.

"We never have pop at our house," Frankie said as he chose 7UP.

"We don't either," said Grace. "My dad won't let us. He calls it sweetened paint thinner, you know, toxic. But my mom drinks it all the time." She pictured ants swarming on the empty bottles next to Bernadette's lawn chair in the backyard.

They sat on the curb, drinking pop. Two kids rode by on their bikes and stared at them. A girl across the street sat reading on a porch swing. Grace looked down the street into town. Even the air felt lazy. What would it be like to live here? Would you feel more confined or freer? Could you find a best friend anywhere? A boyfriend?

"Do you want to buy something to eat?" Frankie said. "We can go to that little park."

"I'm not really hungry," Grace said, because she wasn't. Her stomach was filled with flutters.

"Let's just walk around a little bit and head back. I don't want to get on the wrong side of your dad."

They stood up. Once again, Frankie took her hand. "I like you, Grace," he said. "I mean, I really like you."

A pickup truck pulled into the gas station, and its two doors slammed as a man and a woman got out. Then quiet descended again. Frankie deserved a response. What kind of response? "I watch for you every minute." "I pretend you're with me when you're not." "Ditto."

"Me too," she said.

They started to walk. Two figures moved into Grace's view, far down Main Street where the cluster of stores stood. The smaller person was about half the size of the larger one, who loped ahead and returned. They shrank as they moved farther and farther away, until they must have turned a corner. The sight of Gunda, next to her mother, wasn't as distressing as Grace's first look at her. Was it the distance? Or didn't Gunda have the same shock value once you had seen her up close?

Grace recalled Gunda's hand on Hilda's head, groping for safety. She wondered how long it had been since she had touched Bernadette's head. But that was a ridiculous thought. She was thirteen years old. You didn't pat your mother's head when you were thirteen.

She turned and smiled at Frankie. He smiled back. Grace considered telling him about Hilda and Gunda. Instead she said, "Tell me about your dog."

15

race heard Chuck yelling even before she and
Frankie turned off the main road and onto the long
driveway that led to the two cabins. The yelling stopped
abruptly. Dad's here, Grace reassured herself. Everything
will run more smoothly.

"Your dad seems a lot different from your mom,"
Frankie said.

Grace had always hoped that Bernadette appeared
more normal than she really was to other people.

"I know," she said. "It really messed with my head when
I was a kid."

"That they were different from each other?"

"No, that Bernadette was different from other moms."

"You could see that?"

"If the little kids were asleep or something, she let us
do whatever we wanted so that she could do what she
wanted—mostly nothing. Chuck and Polly and I were on
our own. My best friend Margaret's mother was really

strict. So I knew the difference. Anyway, I had to watch the kids. A lot."

"Why didn't Chuck have to?"

"I think I stepped into it because it made me feel grownup when I was younger. Chuck wasn't as good at it. He burned the food, that kind of thing."

Frankie didn't respond.

"Bernadette did the grocery shopping most of the time. And sometimes, when you would think she'd be mad, she wasn't. Once Chuck put a couple of mice in our neighbors' car and waited."

"What happened?"

"The son had just gotten his driver's license. He got in the car and pulled away from the curb before he saw the mice. Then he hit the gas instead of the brake. He wrecked the wheel."

"And your mom really didn't get mad?"

"Not so much. My dad was the one who took Chuck to the neighbors' to settle up."

Beth came out of the cabin. "Daddy saw you," she said, a smile on her pale face with the pointy chin. "He's here now. He told us that he saw you."

"That's right, Bethie. Are you happy that Dad is here?" When they all got older, it would be Beth, innocent and gentle, who would take care of Dad after Bernadette burned herself to death smoking in bed.

"Come in and see Daddy," Beth said.

"Do you want to go out again?" Frankie asked Grace. "Soon?"

"Sure. There's a lot of road up here."

That wasn't what she wanted to say. Her pores soaked up the sunshine. The warm wind made her ponytail dance just a little. All because of him. How could you tell someone that after one walk?

"That's for sure," Frankie said, looking around as if surveying endless highways. "I'll be seeing you."

He didn't move. He hadn't held her hand since they had turned into the driveway. But he still seemed to have some part of her.

"Great," said Grace.

"Okay."

"Okay. Bye."

Inside the cabin, the only noise was the tinkling of ice in Bernadette's cocktail. Dad looked up from the newspaper that lay open on the table.

"Where is everybody?" Grace asked.

"Pinky and Beth just went down to the beach with Polly and Chuck," Dad said. "I'm going down there in a few minutes."

"How was your love walk, Gracie?" Bernadette said.

Grace ignored the question, which felt like dirty dishwater on her. The kids' voices drifted up from the beach.

"Why did you marry her?" she wanted to ask Dad. "How could you have been so foolish?" But would she want to hear the answer? Besides, if Dad hadn't married Bernadette, she, Grace wouldn't exist. That was a truly horrible thought.

"I'm going down to the beach, too," Grace said.

"I'll go with you," said Dad. He folded the newspaper and walked around the table to squeeze Bernadette's shoulder.

Grace turned and walked through the porch. Dad caught up with her before she reached the steps to the beach.

"How are you doing?" he said.

"I'm going to say it. I've never said it before. I don't understand how you can stand Bernadette." She started crying. If Dad tried to hug her, she would bolt. This wasn't a hugging time.

Dad didn't say anything for a minute or so. "I'm not sure that I understand it myself. I fell for her. She had a lackadaisical way that was very appealing." He paused. "She is, for better or for worse, my wife."

Grace resisted the urge to look at him.

"You get the brunt of it, Gracie. I know that. I don't know what else to do. I wouldn't mind being the at-home parent, but someone has to go to work."

Grace remained silent.

"I'm sorry, Grace."

Grace sat in the woods by herself instead of going down to the beach with Dad. It would feel good to hate him. But she couldn't.

16

That night, Dad made hamburgers that were big enough to meet the edges of the buns he had brought. Polly peeled potatoes next to him.

"I hope those are going to be fried," Chuck said as he came in from a brief fishing trip with Frankie.

"C'mon, Chuck," replied Dad, lifting a knife out of the drawer. "You can chop. Otherwise we won't have this meal ready until tomorrow morning."

"What about Grace?" Chuck asked, casting a frown at her as he walked slowly to the counter. "Why doesn't she have to do anything?"

"How do you do that?" Grace retorted. "Make your nose look like a pig's?"

Chuck began to move toward her. Dad said something to him in a low voice. Chuck took the knife from Dad and began chopping onions.

Grace imagined that Dad had whispered, "Put a mouse turd under the potatoes on her plate." More likely, it was,

"Be bigger than that," or "You're the only one who can let her get to you." Dad knew how to elevate the wronged person and deflate the aggressor.

"I'll set the table," Grace said as an apology to Dad. No one had set the table all week.

"Oh, Daddy, you're making hamburgers," Beth exclaimed happily, entering from the front yard, where she and Pinky had been playing.

"It smells so good," said Pinky, who followed Beth into the cabin. "I'm hungry."

This is what a real family is like, Grace thought: people making food and planning to eat it. There was no Beth crying about a lost puppy. No Polly blinking back tears because Bernadette didn't have candles for the pyramid of Hostess Twinkies that she called a birthday cake. No Pinky worrying about who would sew his elf costume for the school play. A nice parent gave chores to little kids. Little kids liked to be helpful. But they didn't like to be their own parents.

"Those onions could wake up the dead," Bernadette said, emerging from a short nap in her room. "I swear someone stuffed them up my nose."

Grace watched Polly at her potato-peeling station and wondered if she had forgiven Bernadette for leaving her behind at Gunda's. Bernadette had really outdone herself that day.

"Mom, why don't you ever do this?" Polly asked, her peeler held like a question mark in the air.

"Do what? Stink up the house?"

"Bernadette, you know that you want those onions with your burger," Dad said jokingly, without looking up.

"Why, Mom?" Polly continued, as if Dad hadn't spoken. "Why does Dad cook and you don't?"

Chuck turned from the chopping block to stare at Polly. The little kids watched Bernadette, who lit a cigarette and inhaled sharply, as if preparing a response in her lungs.

Dad scooped up more ground meat as he looked at Polly.

"Your mother hates cooking," he said, as if Bernadette weren't in the room. "I can't make her like it. Period."

"That's not a very good answer," Polly said quietly.

"Bernadette, what do you have to say?" said Dad. "Anything to tell the kids?"

"Guilty as charged," she said through her exhalation.

"She made me a sandwich for lunch yesterday," Beth told everyone.

"Redeemed!" Dad said, although he didn't look as happy as his voice sounded. "Let's hurry up and get this dinner on the table."

17

Mom is a little, you know, better today," Polly said to Grace as they sat on the beach on Sunday afternoon.

"She's been awake all day, if that's what you mean."

"I guess so."

Bernadette sat on a lawn chair in the cabin's front yard. Pinky and Beth, playing old maid on the grass near her, chattered brightly, their voices stirring the air.

"She got dressed in the morning, too," said Polly.

"We shouldn't count on it happening again."

"Do you think it's because Dad is here?"

Grace tipped her face back. The sun seemed to be blessing her. Or maybe she felt lighthearted because she wasn't making someone's lunch. "She never acts any different when he's at home," she said. "Maybe she actually misses him."

"Do you know what I thought you would say, Grace?"

"What?"

"Don't expect a miracle."

"I'm surprised I didn't say that, Polly. Very good line."

The girls looked at the lake. In the distance, a boat bobbed on the water. Dad and Frankie's dad and grandpa had gone back out after dropping Pinky off with his catch. At the end of the dock, Frankie and Chuck held their fishing poles as they talked, periodically attempting to push each other into the water. They had fished in Grandpa Ernest's boat with the dads before anyone else was up.

Grace felt Polly's eyes on her. "What is it, Pol?" she said, lowering herself back onto the beach towel. She hated it when Polly got serious on her. Polly had no protective shell.

"Do you ever think that Mom shouldn't have had kids?"

"Polly, that's no way for a Catholic to talk."

"Maybe she could have been something else."

"What? A kindergarten teacher?"

"Grace, don't make fun of me," Polly said. "Not a teacher. Mom likes to joke with people, sleep during the day." She paused. "Maybe she should have been a bartender instead of a mother."

Grace opened her eyes. "I'll give you that one, Polly."

Late in the afternoon, Grace and Frankie took the walk they had planned earlier in the day.

"Your dad is a really nice guy," Frankie said, as they turned onto the road and headed in the opposite direction from their first walk.

"He is."

"He agreed with Grandpa that we should all come up here together next year. Everybody."

"Your mom and brother, too?"

"Sure."

Bernadette and Frankie's mom in neighboring cabins? Even though she couldn't imagine Frankie's mother, Grace excised that situation from her mind immediately.

They joined hands and swung them loosely.

"We're all eating together tonight, but you know that," Grace said.

"Right. I always liked coming to the cabin. It was always great, no matter who else from my family was along. But this is so much better, having your family here and doing stuff all the time." He stopped walking. "But you, here, it's just, you know, over the top."

Their hands stopped swinging as they looked at each other, grasshoppers and cicadas creating the only conversation. Then a faint noise grew louder. They turned in the direction of the footsteps.

Pinky panted behind them, his face pinker than ever with exertion. "Dad said that I could walk with you if I could catch you." He stopped running and walked bent at the waist, his arms wagging in front of him, while he caught his breath.

"What about the rest of your gang?" Frankie said, winking at Grace. "Didn't they want to come, too?"

"No, just me. Where are we going?"

Frankie moved away from Grace to let Pinky in between them. Then Grace and Frankie, without a word, each took one of Pinky's hands and, on the count of three, lifted him as they walked and swung him back and forth as he screamed with delight.

Part of Grace wanted to pound Pinky into the ground. But the larger part couldn't help laughing because Pinky, oblivious to romance, had never looked more alive with joy.

18

After supper, everyone stayed on the beach. Groups formed, broke apart, and re-formed. Grace and Frankie were a popular splinter group, as at least one of the little kids always followed them. Dad was a popular attraction as well.

"Things will settle down when your dad goes," Frankie told Grace. "We still have almost a whole week."

On Monday morning, Dad walked through the main room with his suitcase. His heavy footsteps, in tandem with the sunlight that probed Grace's eyelids, woke her up. Dad leaned over Chuck's bed and said a few words. Grace sat up before Dad reached her. She followed him outside, where the air was the same temperature as her skin. The birds trilled about how happy they were to be birds. Polly sat in her pajamas on the hood of the car. Grace trailed Dad to the trunk. He was wearing a suit.

"You're driving straight to work from here?" she asked.

Dad made a show of slowly lifting his watch to eye

level. "Looks as if my vacation ends"—he paused—"right about now."

"I wish you didn't have to go. Everything is better when you're here."

"Next year, we'll plan this better. I'll be here for the whole time."

Polly slid down from the hood and plodded to the back of the car, stopping in front of Dad. She looked like a beagle—sad-eyed and droopy—who needed a pat on the head.

"Grace, I want you to do something for me while you're here," Dad said, rubbing the top of Polly's head.

"Sure, what?"

"Remember that your sister is not the enemy."

Grace rolled her eyes.

"What goes around comes around," Dad continued.

"I don't need her," Polly said in a sad voice.

"You do, and you will," Dad said. He turned to face Grace. "You'll need her, too, Gracie."

Grace didn't detect anything funny or veiled in his words or face. He was serious. "The others," he continued, "you'll need them, too, now and as you get older. They're your base."

The thought of an adult Chuck disturbed Grace.

Polly sniffled, a prelude to sobs. To her credit, she didn't blurt out a litany of crimes committed against her by Grace.

"You'll be okay, Polly," Dad said, giving her a rocking hug. "I miss you, too."

How could Dad stand Polly, so easily defeated, so weak? Maybe he felt sorry for her because he had a soft spot for the underdog. Maybe he felt sorry for her because she would never be as strong as Grace.

"I love you, Pol," said Dad. "I'll see you soon.

"Love you, too, Gracie," he said as he hugged her. "That Frankie seems like a nice kid." He lowered himself into the driver's seat. "Here's my nickel's worth of advice. Don't do anything you wouldn't want us to know about."

Grace's blush rushed up from her neck as she thought of Dad's eyes on her hand in Frankie's. She promised herself to forget what Dad had just said. It was worse than Bernadette flinging a half-empty box of sanitary napkins on Grace's bed when she was eleven and didn't know what they were.

"Right," she said. "See you soon."

"Love you girls. Chin up, Polly," he said to her, holding her hand through the car window for a moment.

Polly lapped it up like the little puppy that she was, breaking into a smile with her lips pressed together to keep from grinning. No wonder she was so vulnerable, Grace thought, out there in the world with ticker tape on her face broadcasting her thoughts.

Dad turned the key in the ignition with one hand and saluted the girls with the other. As the car rolled off the dirt patch next to the station wagon, Dad waved goodbye. Grace and Polly watched the car until it disappeared in the distance. Grace looked back at the empty spot where the car had been. Beyond it, in front of his cabin, Frankie stood looking at her.

19

*G*race's stomach did a flip.

"Hey, Grace."

"Hi, Frankie." Grace wore the summer pajamas that her grandma, Dad's mom, had made. The pajamas covered everything that a bathing suit covered, but Grace felt strange outside in them. Was it the white eyelet trim or the pajamas themselves?

"What are you doing today?" he said. "We don't have a plan yet."

"You and your dad?"

"No, us." Frankie walked across his mowed lawn to the bramble along the side of Grace's cabin. "Hi, Polly."

"Hi," Polly replied, drying her eyes with the back of her hand.

"Do you want to go to town with Grandpa and me?" he asked Grace.

"Sure, when?"

"Chuck and I were supposed to go fishing this morning, if he gets up, and then my dad and I are going to get some stuff done around the cabin. So, after lunch?"

Polly made a gravelly noise in her throat as she looked at Grace. Grace stared at her, hoping she would disappear. Polly's next noise was raspier.

"Polly, have you been eating pebbles?" Grace said.

"You heard Dad," Polly said in a hiss. "Take me, too."

Grace looked at Frankie, who had turned to examine the front of his cabin. "Dad didn't mean that you're supposed to shadow me at all times," Grace said in a low voice.

"He said you should stick with me."

"When the time is right. You aren't supposed to be a leech," Grace whispered, annoyance rising in her chest. "You need to watch the kids when I'm not here," she added, trying to strike a mature tone.

"I do not," Polly mouthed, hands on her hipbones.

Frankie turned back to face Grace and Polly.

"Maybe this isn't a good day for Grace to go with me," he said.

"It's a great day for me," Grace said, battling the acid creeping into her voice.

"I guess Polly could come, too," he said, as if testing the thought out loud.

"See?" Polly said to Grace.

"You have to watch Pinky and Beth. You can't come with us."

"I suppose if you both come, the other kids could come, too," said Frankie.

Desperation gripped Grace. "We won't all fit in your car."

Frankie's eyes moved upward as if a seating chart was lodged in his forehead. "I think we can," he said.

"Stay here," said Grace. "I'll check with Bernadette."

Grace quietly went inside the cabin, making sure that the screen door didn't bounce. She couldn't get rid of Polly today, but she could block the others from coming along on the outing. Chuck snored softly on his bed. As Grace took hold of his ear, Chuck's eyes opened.

"You're volunteering to play with the little kids so they don't want to go to town with me," she whispered.

Chuck blinked several times. His expression shifted from startled to defiant. "Don't have to," he said.

Grace grasped his ear more firmly. "There's five dollars in it for you if you don't give me any lip, starting this second. I drop one dollar from the deal for every word you say."

Chuck nodded, the side of his face rubbing the pillow.

"As soon as Pinky and Beth get up, tell them that you're all going on a hike or something this afternoon, just the three of you," Grace said. Maybe she was too desperate. Five dollars was almost half of her money, saved with effort from the occasional dollar tucked in a birthday card or from mowing a lawn or babysitting.

"Up you go," she said to Chuck, releasing his ear. "Three dollars when I leave, the rest when I come back."

Now sitting, Chuck scowled. "What should I do with the kids?"

"I told you. Take them on a hike. Pick flowers. Or fish from Frankie's dock. Make a sand city. Just keep them busy."

"You're going to town?"

"Yes."

"What about Polly?"

"She's coming with us."

"What if I want to go, too?"

"This isn't about you. It's a bribe. Take it. Who else is offering you five dollars?"

"All right. But just this once," he said, frowning. "Next time, I want more money."

"Next time?" said Grace. "I hope I never have to make another deal with you."

20

The hours dragged with Dad gone and the long wait for Frankie. Did he have a specific time in mind when he said "after lunch"?

At eleven-thirty, Grace put cereal and milk on the table for the second time that day. She didn't feel up to making a mound of sandwiches. Leaning out the door, she yelled to Pinky and Beth, who were playing tic-tac-toe in the sand on the beach while Polly watched.

"You, too, Polly," she called, torn between duty and resentment.

At the table, Beth spoke softly as Grace leaned over to pour milk on her little sister's cereal. "We're going to play with Chuckie after lunch," she said.

"That's great. What are you going to do?"

"We're going fishing," Pinky said, glowing with excitement. "In a boat."

"Then we're going to clean the fish," added Beth. "I mean, Chuckie cleans the fish. We watch him so that we can learn how to do it." She looked as pleased as if she had just decapitated them herself.

"You've never rowed anything before this summer," Grace said to Chuck, who was trying to juggle two rubber balls. "Are you sure you should take them out? What if it's windy?"

Chuck picked up the balls from the floor and moved over to Grace. In a conspiratorial voice, he said, "I'm tying the boat up to the dock with a lot of slack."

"Make sure they wear life jackets and T-shirts so they don't fry in the sun." Grace had to get the last word in. But Chuck had considered safety. She didn't have to feel so guilty about leaving them.

At noon, Frankie knocked on the cabin door. Bernadette was reading a magazine on the porch.

"Hi, Frankie, which one are you here for?" she said.

"Grace and Polly. We're going to town with my grandpa."

"Grace," Bernadette called. "No one asked me."

"Chuck's going to watch the kids," Grace said, her voice carrying through the window. She patted her pockets to make sure that her comb and remaining money were there.

"Chuck?" Bernadette asked loudly. "Chuck who?"

"C'mon, Ma," Chuck yelled. "I'm the oldest."

Bernadette turned to look at Frankie through the screen door. "How are you getting there?"

"My grandpa will drive us."

"Bagley or Ravensville?"

"Just Bagley."

"I thought you kids could walk there."

Frankie paused. "My grandpa is driving because he wants to find some old friend in town. He said that we could walk around and get a cone and stuff while he visits."

"Let's go," Grace said to Polly with a murderous look. She wanted to escape. Why was Bernadette interrogating Frankie? Was that her idea of conversation?

"Bye, kids," Grace said.

Grace walked quickly to the car, opened the back door, and reached for Frankie's hand to pull him in with her. It was a bold move, but necessary. "Get in front," she mouthed to Polly, who had run around to the other back door, which was mercifully locked.

With her trademark about-to-cry expression, Polly opened the front passenger door and slowly got into the car. Grace almost felt sorry for her, then bristled at the thought of how Polly had invited herself.

Grandpa Ernest sat behind the wheel in a short-sleeved checkered shirt with a starched collar. He didn't have much hair, but there was enough to show comb marks.

"Frankie's a lucky guy to have you girls around," Grandpa said as he began to drive, "and your brother, too. I hope you kids come up here every summer now that the cabin is Bernadette's." He looked in the rearview mirror and caught Grace's eye.

"Maybe we will," she said. Why would Bernadette care where her family vacationed as long as she had a carton of cigarettes, somewhere to sleep, and a surrogate mother for the kids?

"It's wonderful to have neighbors next door again," said Grandpa.

Experimentally, Grace put her hand on the seat as she watched the trees roll by. Like a warm suction cup, Frankie's hand attached itself to hers.

21

Grandpa dropped Grace, Frankie, and Polly off at Icey Ices. "There's a park a little farther down Main Street," he said. "It has a swimming pool built into the ground."

"I know the park, Grandpa," Frankie said. "I used to go wading in that pool."

"The girls will want to see the town. That's part of the tour."

"Thanks for the ride," Grace said.

Polly muttered something unintelligible and slipped out her door.

"I'll pick everyone up here in, say, an hour and a half," Grandpa said. "I'm looking up an old friend who may or may not be in. Wish me luck."

"Okay," said Frankie. "Thanks for the lift."

Grace wished that they had agreed to walk back. Now they were stuck waiting for Grandpa. But maybe the walk would have been too long with Polly.

At the Icey Ices counter, Frankie stood firm. "Grandpa gave me money for everyone. So order whatever you like."

Polly looked troubled, as if wondering whether "everyone" included her.

"Did Grandpa mean Polly, too?" Grace said.

"Don't listen to her, Polly," Frankie said with a wink.

This could turn ugly. Grace had seen what happened when two kids who didn't know each other ganged up on a third person they both knew well. The twosome created a bond at the expense of the popular one, which would be her. She had to rise above it and treat Polly as if she were a real person.

"I bet you'll get a strawberry cone," Grace said to her sister. "I'm almost tempted to get one, too."

"That's what I *am* getting," Polly said. A flicker of pleasure crossed her face.

"Chocolate for me," Grace told the girl behind the screen.

"Single or double?"

"Double."

"Could I have my strawberry ice cream in a root beer float?" Polly asked Frankie. "Would that cost too much?"

"Nope. Grandpa said to get whatever you want."

The counter girl looked at them as if they mattered less than the gum she was smacking.

"I'll have a root beer float, too," Frankie said. "With vanilla."

The girl turned her back, sighing as she dug her scoop into the chocolate ice cream.

"We might as well walk over to the park," Frankie said when everyone's order had been filled by the gum chewer. "We can cool our feet off in the kiddie pool."

They moved along the sidewalk, the sun baking their bodies. Grace hadn't considered the rate at which the sun would melt her ice cream in a cone. The napkins wrapped around it were damp with chocolate before Grace finished the top scoop, no matter how fast she licked the sides. Chocolate began to drip from the cone onto her hand. She held back, walking slower than the others as she tried to stem the flow of the chocolate river.

Soon they were in front of the grocery store that Bernadette hadn't taken them to the week before. The store would have a restroom, or at least a water fountain, where Grace could rinse off.

"I'm stopping here for a minute," Grace said, holding her streaked forearm behind her. "I'll catch up."

"What's the matter with your arm?" Polly asked.

"Nothing is the matter with my arm."

"Why are you hiding it?"

"I'm not hiding it."

"Where's your ice-cream cone?"

Behind her back, Grace shifted the soggy cone from her sticky hand to her clean one. She held the cone in front of her as if presenting Polly with a bouquet. "Please, Pol, try to think about something other than my cone. If you wanted one, you should have said so. I'm going inside to use the bathroom, if you must know."

Polly looked embarrassed at the mention of the word "bathroom" in front of Frankie.

"Go on, you two. I'll catch up in a flash."

"We'll save a swing for you," Frankie said.

"See you there." Grace pushed the grocery store door open. A cashier stood at the end of one of two checkout lanes, a flyswatter poised above her head. Her mouth was tight.

"Is there a restroom?" Grace asked as she walked toward the woman.

"Customers only."

"I'm a customer," Grace said, dropping her cone into a trash can. "Or do you only wait on flies?"

The woman looked at Grace with disdain. "Past the charcoal," she said. "Last door on the right."

"Thank you ever so much," said Grace. She imagined finding a hundred-dollar bill on the bathroom floor. After that, she would pick through the penny candy and buy one of something that cost two for a penny. If she had more time, she would read all the comics on display until the cashier threatened her.

In the restroom, the towel on the roller looked as if it

hadn't been changed since it was installed. Grace scanned the room for paper towels. No luck. She turned on the faucet, and cold water ran out of a single spigot. Leaning over the basin, she moved her arm back and forth while she rubbed it clean with her left hand.

Had Bernadette ever been in this restroom when she was thirteen? It was an unsettling thought. Maybe Bernadette had seen the same towel. Grace dried her hand and arm on her shorts.

A fly buzzed around her head as she pushed the door to exit. Grace shooed the fly with her hand. The door resisted as if someone was standing on the other side. Ignoring the fly, Grace shoved the door with both hands until there was an opening almost big enough to slip through.

On the other side of the door was a woman with a soft, broad body in a plaid housedress. The startled woman, her face framed in looping brown-gray curls, stared at Grace.

For a moment, Grace felt frozen in a dream in which she couldn't run but only mimic movement in ponderous slow motion. Then she pushed harder and smelled mingled liniment and sweat as she moved through the door. She was torn between the desperation to flee and the obligation to be kind.

"Hello, Gunda," she said. Then Grace walked stiffly away from the frightened Gunda and past the two check-out lanes.

"You said you were a customer," the cashier called, waving her arm as if she would reel Grace in with the fly-swatter.

From the back of the store, a crackling voice called, "Gunda, where are you? I'm here, dear!"

22

*F*rankie and Polly sat on swings, their backs to Grace. She tried to control her breathing as she walked over the grass to them. Moving slowly and hoping that her heartbeat would follow suit, she took in the sweetness: the white bubble of a bandshell; bobbing snapdragons and lilies and pansies planted by the Interlude Garden Club, according to the hand-painted sign; the wading pool guarded by a watchful and weather-beaten sculpted sea horse.

As she drew close, she paused at a water fountain that burbled when she stepped on the foot pedal. The noise alerted Polly and Frankie, who turned in their swings, the chains crossing in front of them.

"What's new in downtown Bagley?" Frankie said.

"A new generation of flies."

Frankie laughed and, for a moment, Grace relaxed.

Then Polly spoke. "Grace, why are you so pale under your blusher?"

"Pale?" She never wore makeup, but today she had lifted Bernadette's cosmetic pouch from her purse and brushed her freckled cheekbones with blusher, then smoothed the edges with toilet paper to blend it.

Now Frankie stared.

"Pale," Polly repeated.

Blurting it out would be a relief. "I saw Gunda, Polly, up close. You saw her once. But this was my second time, third, actually, if you count the long view. She has Bernadette's eyes, a deep, velvety brown. Beth's eyes, too." But, of course, Grace couldn't say that.

"I'm just so hot," she said. It was too much to explain.

"Don't people turn red when they're hot?" Polly said.

"Speaking of people, why are we the only people here?" Grace said.

"My mom worries about heatstroke," Frankie said. "I bet people bring their little kids out when the sun is lower."

"Let's go for a dip," Grace said. "We might as well enjoy all of Bagley's little attractions."

The water in the pool reached the bottom of Grace's knees.

"The only thing to do with this water is race in it," she said. "First, the skipping competition."

The bottom of the pool was slick.

"Help!" Polly screamed when she lost her balance, but she stayed upright.

"Victory!" Frankie yelled when he touched the other side, but Grace felt the pool's edge at the same time.

"You're louder than me," she said. "That's why you think you won."

"Ask the photographer for the proof. Someone is covering this event, right?"

"I disqualify you."

"On what basis?"

"For acting like my brother."

"What's the next race?" Frankie said. "You choose since you're the Olympic committee."

"Okay. We're going to crawl."

"Grace, that will hurt our knees," said Polly.

"Just for a minute."

They lined up, and Polly said, "On your mark, get set, go!"

Polly pulled ahead quickly, assuming the position of a dog swimming with a stick in its mouth. Grace couldn't resist the urge to call over the splashing, "I think you've found your sport, Polly."

Grace won the hopping race, and Frankie won the running backward contest. After that they tried to step on each other's toes.

"Let's go lie on the grass," Polly said, hopping and cradling her foot. "We can take turns telling what animals the clouds look like."

"I'm going to that grocery store for some pop first," Frankie said. "What do you two want?"

"Orange Crush," said Polly.

"Tahitian Treat."

"Should I get some comics?" Frankie asked. "We still have more than half an hour before Grandpa shows up."

"Perfect," Grace said. She lay on the grass, hands behind her head. A towering maple shaded her from the sun's glare. With every breath she took, Grace relaxed. Gunda was under Hilda's control. Comics were on the way. Even though Polly was in tow, Grace was in town because Frankie had asked her.

23

"Grace, are you still mad that I came along?" Polly's voice floated over the soft swishy noises in the grass.

"No," Grace said. She didn't want to discuss Polly's stupid question.

"Are you sure?"

"Yes." It took a lot of energy to talk when you were taking a nap.

"But you've been acting kind of mad."

Grace didn't answer Polly. Instead, she imagined being a kid who didn't have to take care of her siblings. This could be her life: lazing in the grass, reading outside, letting the breeze ruffle her hair. But these times were rare, spoiled by the need to wash clothes so that everyone had clean underwear.

On the other side of the park, a car door slammed. Grace sat up and watched an old man emerge and walk around a car that looked like Grandpa Ernest's. He opened the passenger door. Polly trained her eyes on the man, too.

"He's pretty spry for a grandpa," she said.

"He *is* a grandpa. Frankie's."

Frankie's Grandpa Ernest was helping Hilda, the human pretzel, emerge from the passenger seat.

"Why?" asked Polly, distress in her voice. "Why is he with her?"

They watched Grandpa Ernest walk Hilda to the nearest park bench and help her sit. Grandpa returned to the car, but Gunda had already opened the back door. She got out and looked from side to side. Hilda called to her, and Gunda joined her mother and stood there listening for a few seconds. Then she moved away, repeatedly bending down to pluck something from the ground.

"Dandelions," Polly whispered. "I think she's picking dandelions."

Grandpa sat down next to Hilda on the bench.

"Do you think that she's the friend he came to see?" Polly asked in a voice filled with disbelief.

"He said it was an old friend," Grace said. "Hilda qualifies as old."

"But wouldn't he try to get out of it when he saw her?"

"Maybe he's too nice. What could he say, 'I changed my mind. You're too twisty'?"

"That's my grandpa over there," said Frankie as he approached. "Who's with him?"

"That's my mom's aunt."

"Last night Grandpa said he wanted to surprise his old friend." Frankie stared across the park. "He never said it was a woman."

"That's her daughter," Grace said. "My mom's cousin."

"Oh," said Frankie. "From here, she doesn't look like your mom."

"You're right about that," Grace said, jolted by the inanity of Frankie's remark. But if Gunda pulled her hair back and wore pedal pushers and smoked and didn't have a baggy body, Frankie would see her differently. If, that is, she hadn't been underwater too long.

"Frankie, why would your grandpa be checking up on Hilda now? Doesn't he come up every summer?"

"Beats me. Maybe because he didn't think of it while my grandma was alive? When Grandpa told you guys about hiding in the woods when Hilda got married and stuff, maybe he started thinking about her again. He wouldn't really have run into her on water skis at the lake or anything."

Grace tried to straighten the sequence out in her head. Grandpa Ernest could have gotten Hilda's address from Bernadette. Or he might have known where Hilda lived in this little town. Hilda didn't have a phone, so he couldn't tell her that he was stopping by. When Grandpa arrived, Hilda and Gunda had been at the grocery store. He waited for them in front of the house. Grace could imagine

Grandpa helping Hilda put the groceries away. Then he brought them to the park.

"I got the comics and the pop," Frankie said. Grace realized that neither she nor Polly had remembered why Frankie had left.

Grace flipped through the pile that Frankie pulled from under his arm. "These are good," she said. She took three and held the rest in front of Polly. Looking horrified, Polly was fixated on Gunda, who seemed to be collecting all the dandelions in the park.

"Pol, look, Frankie got *Little Lulu*," she said. "He must have read your mind. Sit down with me and read."

Frankie positioned himself against the trunk of the maple tree. "It doesn't look as if Grandpa's in a hurry," he said. "Pick your spot."

"Why doesn't your grandpa see us if we can see him?" Polly asked, still staring.

"I guess he's not interested in looking around," Frankie replied. "I mean, he seems to be more interested in your relative." He started reading the *Archie* comic.

Grace remembered her walk to town and back with Frankie. How simple that was, only the two of them.

"Grace," Polly said quietly, "I can't concentrate with her running around like that."

"Really, Polly, what can she do to us? Pick our dandelions?"

"I'm so afraid of her."

"What am I supposed to do? I let you tag along and you act like a baby."

"Okay, Gracie." Polly sniffled. "She won't come over here. I'm okay. See, I'm okay."

Why me? Grace said to herself. She willed Polly to vaporize.

"What's the matter?" asked Frankie, looking up from the comic.

"That Gunda woman, the one who's running around, scares Polly."

Frankie looked past Grace to Polly, whose face was now in her hands.

"Polly," Frankie said in a coaxing-a-kitten-out-of-its-hiding-place voice. "Hey, Polly."

Polly splayed her fingers and peeked at Frankie.

"She won't come over here. She's totally happy over there."

"She makes me so nervous."

Frankie looked at Grace as if expecting an explanation of Polly's behavior.

"Gunda scared Polly once, at Hilda's house," Grace said. "She didn't mean to, but she startled her to death or something." Grace looked at Polly, giving her the opportunity to add to or modify this interpretation. Polly stared in Gunda's direction, eyes wide with fear. Grace looked for herself.

Walking with purpose, Gunda moved in a straight line

toward the seated sisters. She was a giant growing larger and larger as she trod over the grass, her hand extended. Gunda halted abruptly in front of Polly, who appeared to have turned to stone, and presented her with a bouquet of dandelions and clover.

A word gurgled out of Gunda's throat like a broken growl. "Girl," she pronounced over Polly. "Girl."

Polly did not move. Grace reached up and put her hand around the stems that escaped from the bottom of Gunda's fist. "I'll give them to her, to the girl," she said. Gunda released the flowers.

As Gunda retreated, Grandpa Ernest crossed the park.

"Hello!" he called, waving a long, stout branch that he used as a third leg. "How long have you been lounging here for?"

"For a while," Frankie answered. "What are you doing here, Grandpa? Are you on a date?"

"You noticed that I'm not alone," Grandpa said. "What's the matter with little Polly?" He held his walking stick over Polly as if she were a lifeless bug that he might prod.

"She's just a quiet one," Grace said.

"Are you certain that she's all right?"

Polly, who had been looking at the ground, tipped her head back so that she could see Grandpa Ernest. She stared as if wondering whether Gunda had morphed into this familiar visage.

"Are you feeling under the weather, Polly?" Grandpa Ernest inquired. "Would you like a drink of water?"

"She's fine." Grace pointed at Polly's Orange Crush. "Are you having a nice time with Hilda?"

"We're having a *wonderful* time. It's a marvelous day when you have someone with whom to enjoy so many memories."

No one could summon a reply to this declaration from Grandpa Ernest, who had voluntarily sat on a park bench with an ancient pocket-size woman.

"Did she know you were going to show up?" Frankie said, breaking the silence.

"Oh, no. After Bernadette visited Hilda, I wondered why I hadn't done so myself. Over the years, my Julie and I would sometimes run into Hilda when we came into town. This is the first year I've returned since my Julie died. To proceed, I spied Hilda and her daughter on their way home from a little shopping trip, so the timing was perfect."

Another silence followed, during which Grace pictured Grandpa Ernest cutting his losses by fleeing the park.

"The funny thing is," he continued, "Hilda may be a little stooped, but I would know that pretty face anywhere."

Grace glanced at Polly, whose mouth was open in a way that suggested her jaw's hinges were severed.

"I'd better be getting back to them," he said. "Just a few

more minutes here and then I'll drive the girls home. I'll be back to pick you up in about half an hour, if that suits you."

Grace took a moment to grasp who "the girls" were. To Grandpa Ernest, "the girls" were not her and Polly, but Hilda and Gunda. His thinking must be distorted because he was old. "Aging," Grace said to herself. "Avoid it."

Grace, Polly, and Frankie watched Grandpa grow smaller until he was in proportion to Hilda and Gunda, patiently awaiting his return.

"Your cousin made a beeline for you, Polly," Frankie said. "Why would she do that?"

"When Bernadette made us go see them, Polly went into Gunda's room to find some liniment," Grace said. "It was a bet."

"So she recognized you, Polly?" Frankie asked.

"Maybe. I don't know," said Polly, speaking for the first time since Gunda had traversed the park. "It was dark in her room, and light was behind me. She gave the dandelions to me, didn't she?"

"You're her little pet," Grace said.

"It's a curse," Polly said with resignation. "It's the curse of the liniment."

Polly was naming things, Grace thought with agitation. This outing wasn't about Polly. If it had a name, it would be "Grace and Frankie's Golden Summer," not "The Curse of the Liniment."

"Maybe I could break the curse if I gave the liniment back," Polly said, patting the book bag she had carried on her shoulder to the park.

"What? You have it with you?"

"I thought that if we were in town, I might have a chance to leave it on her steps." She sighed. "I didn't really want to, though."

"Polly, you don't even know where she lives." Hilda's house didn't have steps, but Grace decided to let that go.

"It's not a big town."

"Gad, Polly, I'd hate to see what else you're carrying around with you in that thing. Why don't you just give the liniment back now?"

"Gracie, I can't. She scares me too much."

"Then give it to me."

"No, Gracie, don't go over there."

"She won't hurt anyone, Pol," Frankie said. "Look, Grandpa's there. And her mom. She came over here to give you flowers, not strangle you."

The "Pol" thing was too much, Grace thought. Frankie was becoming too familiar with her weakling sister.

"Give me the liniment," Grace commanded.

Polly reluctantly put her hand in the book bag and produced the small pot.

Grace made her feet take turns, one in front of the other, as she moved across the expanse of land. Gunda stared from her post in front of a tree next to the bench where Grandpa Ernest and Hilda sat. When Grace was close enough to see the mole on Gunda's chin, she called, "Hello," and raised her hand in greeting. Grandpa smiled a wide smile and Hilda, a sweet one.

Before Grace knew what was happening, a whoosh flashed past her. She turned to watch Gunda run across the park. Within seconds, Gunda headed back, using a clumsy walk-run to cross the grass.

This time, Gunda was not alone. Arms extended in front of her, she carried Polly, as if presenting a ceremonial flag, or, perhaps, a ninety-two-pound communion wafer. Frankie ran alongside. Gunda, panting heavily, reached the bench and placed Polly next to Grandpa Ernest.

"Whoa!" Grandpa said. "I see that she wants us all together."

"Gunda!" said Hilda, looking surprised. "No picking up children!"

"Girl," Gunda said, dragging out each letter.

No one else spoke until Grace said, "This is yours," to Hilda. "It kind of followed us home accidentally."

"My, my, I looked all over Gunda's room for this," she said. "Look, Gunda, this nice cousin found your liniment."

Gunda patted Polly's head.

"She seems to be very taken with your sister," Hilda said to Grace. "She's a quiet one, isn't she? Just like my Gunda."

"Girl," Gunda said.

With a show of bravery that was painful to witness, Polly raised her head and smiled at Gunda.

Hilda pulled a hankie out of her cardigan sweater sleeve and dabbed at her eyes.

"She so rarely speaks," she said to Polly. "This is the talkingest day we've had in a long, long time."

25

$\mathcal{G}$randpa Ernest drove Hilda and Gunda home and returned to the park for Grace, Frankie, and Polly. Grandpa was the only talkative one. "After all these years, to think that we could pick up as if we had never lost touch," he said. "She's the same fun gal I remember."

Poor man, Grace thought. He's lost his mind and doesn't know it.

Frankie broke the silence in the backseat, where Polly had pushed in next to Grace.

"Grandpa, you already have a girlfriend."

"Dot is a wonderful lady," Grandpa answered. "But there's something special about someone you knew when you were just a pip."

"He has a girlfriend?" Grace said quietly to Frankie.

Grandpa caught Grace's eye in the rearview mirror. "Are you asking about my lady friend?" he asked. "She has a grownup family and grandchildren, too. We love to go dancing. But when I saw Hilda today, she brought my past alive."

Your past doesn't sound that great, Grace thought. Hilda was older than you, and she married someone else.

"Hilda will always represent possibilities to me," Grandpa continued. "Summer, youth, a beautiful lake, a lovely girl on the threshold of womanhood."

Grace looked at Frankie, who raised his eyebrows. Grace raised hers back, making sure that Grandpa wasn't looking at her in the rearview mirror.

"For one afternoon, I forgot my arthritis," he said, "because of Hilda."

Grace stared at the back of Grandpa, his neck a pattern of deep creases that didn't resemble skin. She couldn't think of one thing to say.

"She was thrilled. She was so happy to see me. You already know that I was crushed when she married Harold. But then I found my Julie, and she made me feel the same way that Hilda made me feel. Full of possibility."

Grace looked out the window at the trees. Grandpa was repeating himself. He had already covered possibility. How could you respond to someone who turned crooked little Hilda into a glamorous movie star?

"You don't understand now," he droned on. "But someday you will. Certain people become more precious with time."

What had all that possibility come to? A visit with a crone? Grace stifled a yawn.

Polly shifted in her seat. "Recovering, Pol?" Grace asked.

"She didn't want to hurt me, did she, Grace?"

"I don't think she's a hurting kind of person."

"Hey, Grandpa," Frankie interjected. "Does Gunda hurt people or just scare them?"

"Neither," Grandpa said. "She's just a bit slow."

Grace thought about how Gunda's life was changed by carelessness. Someone had taken their eyes off her. Add bad luck or bad timing. She pictured Beth bobbing on the water. She blinked the image away and noticed Frankie's thigh next to her own. Now, that was easy on the eye. His thigh was leaner than Chuck's and less lanky than Pinky's. During the school year, tweedy uniform pants covered boys' thighs.

"What are you looking at?" Frankie asked.

"Your thigh is hairier and firmer than a girl's," Grace didn't say. "It's not a self-conscious thigh, pushed up just a little from the seat so that the fat doesn't splat out the sides. If you were a girl, we might talk about how thighs can puff over the tops of nylons, especially if there's a girdle pushing from above."

"Nothing," she said. "I wonder if being old feels as bad as it looks."

"Old people kind of dry up," Polly whispered. "That's why their faces crack."

Grandpa Ernest's face had definitely cracked. But his face didn't scare kids. Bernadette had a youngish face, still freckly and fresh in spite of all the kids and cigarettes. But that didn't make her more likable.

"How do you know if kids will like you when you're a grownup?" Grace asked Frankie.

"What are you kids talking about?" said Grandpa.

"Ask him," Grace mouthed.

"Grandpa, how do you know if kids will like you when you're old?"

"I don't think you do. They probably do if you treat them decently. I never thought about it."

"There's a man who lives about two blocks from our school," Grace said. "Kids hate him. Every day after school—even when it's cold outside—he yells at kids if they go near his grass."

"Or his snow," said Polly.

"Right, his snow, too. He looks as if he spends the whole day inside thinking about how kids are out to get him."

"What does he do?" Grandpa asked.

"Shakes his cane. Yells. Says he's going to call the police if you walk too close to his yard."

"I would say that he lashes out because he's so un-happy."

"His poor wife," Polly added. "She waves at me when she's outside gardening and her husband isn't there."

"Polly, you are a kind girl," Grandpa said. "Gunda senses how kind you are. Hilda is kind, too."

Grace looked at Polly, pale at the mention of Gunda. Were kind people losers? Kind Hilda had one date every fifty years or so with a grandpa. The kind wife of the man who waved his cane couldn't be having much fun, either. Dad was kind. But he fell for a cute girl who didn't seem to know that if you had babies, you were responsible for them.

Grandpa turned onto the long driveway that led to the cabins. Grace's head hurt. She wondered if it was too late to become a genuinely nice, kind person, even though the rewards seemed meager. Otherwise, she might turn into Bernadette. That was a horrible thought.

26

In the evening, Grace sat in a lawn chair in front of the cabin, staring at the lake. Beth and Pinky sat on the grass next to her, slowly turning the pages of the new comics that Frankie had let them borrow. Neither of them asked Grace to read the words they didn't know inside the puffy balloons. They were in awe of the new comics.

"Look," Pinky said. "I think the ink is still wet." He held his hand up for Beth and Grace to see. There wasn't any color on his fingers, but Beth nodded solemnly before turning back to her comic.

When Grace had paid Chuck the rest of the five dollars for watching the kids, it hurt. What had she gained? Frankie's hand had rested on hers in the car, his fingers curving around it. But she could have done without the rest of the afternoon: Gunda's heart-stopping appearance at the restroom door, Gunda's lope across the park with Polly flapping in her arms, and Grandpa, who didn't seem to know the difference between fun and prehistoric memories.

She closed her eyes against the setting sun, which warmed her face even as the breeze cooled it. Her thoughts tangled and bumped into each other as she drifted toward sleep. Something stirred, and Grace opened her eyes. Frankie sank onto the grass beside her.

"They like the comics?" he said, nodding at Beth and Pinky, who stared hard at the pages as if Frankie might suddenly snatch their reading away.

"Hooked. They barely noticed that we had dog food for dinner."

He snorted appreciatively. "I was thinking," he said, suddenly businesslike, "that we should have a party. We could invite Hilda and Gunda."

Grace frowned. A party should include her and Frankie and kids their age on the beach, with music blaring from a transistor radio. They would dance in the sand in bare feet and build a fire that they would sit around when the stars came out. Frankie would tell her she looked beautiful with her strawberry blond hair tousled. He wouldn't say "red hair."

"A party?" she repeated.

"We could build a fire and roast hot dogs and marshmallows."

Was Frankie normal? Didn't he know that Bernadette

and Chuck and everyone else she didn't want to see would be on the beach fending off Gunda?

"Wait a minute," she said. "It's your grandpa who wants to have a party, right?"

"Right."

"Grandpa wants a party for Hilda."

"I guess so."

"Why doesn't he just ask her out to the park bench again?"

"I don't know. He told my dad and me that we should have a party with your family on your last night here. That's Thursday, right?"

"Right." Why Bernadette wanted to leave before the weekend was a mystery. Maybe she couldn't last any longer without Dad's cooking. "And he wants to ask Gunda, too?"

"Yup."

"He'd better ask them before they're booked. Why were you acting as if the party was your idea?"

"It's kind of embarrassing," he said, looking at his bare toes, "to have your grandpa so excited about a centenarian."

Poor, poor Grandpa, Grace thought. "We would love to have a party, wouldn't we?" Grace said to Pinky and Beth, who had stopped pretending to read as they eavesdropped.

"We love parties," Beth said, raising her eyes to Frankie and then shyly looking away.

"Okay, a party," said Frankie. "You're in, too, Pinky?"

"Sure," Pinky said, trying to inject a dose of swagger into his thin voice. "And we like the comics, a lot."

"Good, I'm glad," Frankie said as he got up from the ground. He looked at Grace. "Can you go on a walk tomorrow morning after I go fishing with Chuck?"

"Sure," Grace said, feeling herself turn red. Why did that happen when her skin had stayed calm until now? "A walk sounds good."

"A party?" Bernadette said when Grace found her playing solitaire inside at the big table. "I don't think Hilda wants to hang out here."

"Grandpa Ernest will be in charge."

"Since when does he give parties?" said Bernadette, tapping a cigarette out of her pack. "It'll be at his cabin, right?"

"On the beach."

"A beach party with Hilda. Now, that's different."

"Frankie said that Grandpa plans to go into town tomorrow to invite Hilda."

"It would save me from making another trip in to see the old girl," said Bernadette, blowing smoke rings across the table. "Why don't you take money out of my purse and ask Ernest to pick up some chips for us to bring?"

"He wants to buy all the food." She and Polly could make a cake or a pan of brownies. Grace couldn't ask someone else's grandpa to shop for Bernadette.

"I suppose we'll let him," said Bernadette, eyeing Grace with suspicion. "Was this party your idea?"

"No. Grandpa Ernest thought it up."

"So, Thursday night, a blowout. A beach party. Your dad and I used to party at the river."

Grace hated Bernadette's references to herself as a young person. Bernadette—the mother of five kids—mentioned boyfriends from time to time, always a different one. As a girl, she must have had "It." Grace and her friends knew those girls. Often they weren't the prettiest or the funniest or the most popular, but they radiated something special. The girls with "It" were loose and comfortable in their bodies and, without fail, drew boys to them effortlessly. Dad hadn't gotten away.

"All you have to do is show up," Grace said. "Grandpa or Frankie's dad will pick up Hilda and Gunda, I guess."

This wouldn't qualify as a real party. Who wanted a party with an age span from six years old to about one hundred, complete with your mother's cousin who could speak two words? Poor Polly. Gunda would be on the lookout for Girl.

"Count me in," Bernadette said, "but don't sign me up to make punch or anything."

Grace stood. She should round the kids up for bed.

"Bernadette," she said, "I wish Dad could have stayed for this."

"So do I, Gracie."

The words stunned Grace. Bernadette had responded without her trademark edge. Who was this woman?

Bernadette lipped her cigarette as she began to flip through her cards, slapping one down with an accompanying cheer.

An aberration, Grace thought, recalling a spelling word she had never used. An aberration.

27

*I*n her dream, Grace walked with Frankie down an end-less wooded path. The sun worshipped Frankie, high-lighting his hair and casting him in vivid relief against the unbroken blue of the sky.

An unwelcome pattering on the roof woke her. Today was Thursday, a day to walk with Frankie.

"Gracie, what will we do today?" Beth leaned over Grace, her warm breath smelling of toast. "It's raining."

Rain? Rain should be forbidden at cabins. It hadn't rained the entire time they'd been here. Why now?

"I don't know, Bethie," she said. "We'll think of some-thing."

Grace shut her eyes against reality. Tomorrow they would go. She wanted to stay at the cabin as desperately as she had wanted to leave it on the first day.

The light in the cabin was a feeble gray. Pinky sat in a chair by the window, a low-watt bulb in an unshaded lamp providing him with enough illumination to pore over Frankie's comics again.

"What time is it, Pinky?" Grace asked. Pinky looked up, then reached into his T-shirt pocket. He carried a pocket watch that he had found in a church parking lot. In another family, someone would have made him call the Lost and Found. But Grace never said anything because Pinky was so pleased with it.

"It's ten-twelve," he said, snapping the cover shut and returning the watch to his pocket. "Probably ten-thirteen by now."

"We could play games, Gracie," said Beth.

From the other side of the room, Chuck rustled in his bed. "Frankie's cabin has lots of games," he said. "If you can think of a game, they have it."

"Can we ask him if we can come over?" said Polly, hidden in the gloom on the other side of the room.

"It's so neat over there," Grace said. "I don't know if Grandpa Ernest and Frankie's dad want us tracking mud on their floor."

"We could take our shoes off," said Pinky.

"I'll ask," Chuck said, his voice muffled under the covers.

If Chuck asked, it was Chuck's show. Grace racked her brain. She and Frankie had planned to go on a walk. Now the day was turning into a circus. How could she take control back? Did she have to stay up every night making contingency plans?

"Hey, it's darker in here than it is outside," Frankie called from the porch. "Is Grace in there?" Frankie stepped inside the cabin after stomping his feet to discharge some of the water.

Grace pulled the sheet up to her chin as Frankie looked down on her. "Hi," she said, hoping that her sour night breath wouldn't float up to him.

"Grandpa's in the car on his way to go grocery shopping, and he said that I could ask you to come along."

"He's in the car?"

"Yup."

"Will he wait while I get dressed?"

"I guess so. He probably thought that you were, you know, up."

"Give me two minutes."

Frankie surveyed the room. "Hi, Polly. Hi, Pinky. Hi, Beth."

"You go outside," Grace said, still under the sheet. "Then the two minutes start."

Frankie walked over to Chuck and tapped him on the head as if he were knocking at the door. "Hey, big guy, how much beauty sleep do you need?"

When the porch door slammed after Frankie, Grace raced into the bathroom, brushed her teeth, and dressed.

She ran a comb through her hair and pulled it into a ponytail as she moved back into the big room, then ran her hand under the rollaway for her tennis shoes.

"Tell Bernadette I'll be back in a while," she said to Polly. "Did you say something, Bethie?"

"What about the games, Gracie?"

"We'll ask Frankie when I get back, okay?"

"Okay, Gracie."

Grace paused to look at Beth, who gave Grace an expectant smile, equal parts hope and disappointment.

"Okay," Beth repeated softly.

Grace knew what she had to do even though she felt sick with misery. "I'm coming right back," she said to Beth. "I'm not leaving you this morning after all."

She didn't bother to look for a jacket before walking outside into the rain. Frankie opened the back door of the car for her.

"I can't go with you," she said, rain running into her eyes. "I want to, but I can't."

"Will you tell me why later?"

"Yes."

"Should I come over when we get back?"

"Do you think I could bring the kids to your cabin?"

"Sure."

"They want to see your game collection."

Grace backed away from the car and held her hand up in farewell. She didn't want Frankie to think that she was mad at him. Through the rain-blurred window, Frankie waved back. Grandpa tapped the horn two times. Good. Bye.

On the porch, Grace kicked off her shoes and shook her wet head.

"I should have gone with Frankie," Chuck said.

"You could have," Grace said, without stopping. She crossed the big room and paused in the hallway. Cigarette smoke escaped from underneath Bernadette's door.

race's resolve began to falter. But she walked up to Bernadette's door and pushed it open. Bernadette looked up from her magazine and blew smoke out of her nostrils.

"What's up, Gracie?"

Grace didn't have one thing to say. She had a multitude of grievances. But with Bernadette, you had one chance to speak before she would say that you must be having a hell of a day, or blow smoke out of her ears for a laugh, or ask if you were having your period. Grace took two deep breaths to steady herself. She had given up a date with Frankie, even if they were only going into town with Grandpa. Beth and Pinky lived in anticipation of being let down. Dad had gone. That stunk. Everything stunk. Why didn't Bernadette see that?

"I cannot stand how you act," she said to Bernadette, the words rolling out of her mouth as if they had been lined up. "Or maybe I can't stand how you don't act."

"Gracie, Gracie, Gracie," Bernadette said. "You sound like a four-year-old."

"I mean it."

"Did your boyfriend disappear? Is that why your underwear's in a bundle?"

"Don't do that to me. I'm sick of it." Shaking, Grace crossed the room and grabbed her mother's sheet. But instead of dramatically flinging it off Bernadette as intended, Grace released it as soon as she had grasped it. Bernadette stubbed her cigarette out in the bedside ashtray, as though extinguishing Grace's determination.

"Grace, really, I'm minding my own business and you barge in here like a banshee." Bernadette's skin had an unhealthy, pasty look to it. No makeup, Grace realized.

"Mama, I'm just so tired of taking care of everything," she said.

Bernadette pushed her legs out of bed and her feet into their flip-flops. She put her terry-cloth robe over her baby doll pajamas and stuffed a packet of cigarettes into her pocket.

" 'Mama'?" she said to Grace, who was now sitting next to her on the bed. "I haven't heard that word from you in about a hundred years."

"It surprised me, too," Grace muttered, putting her face in her hands.

"I suppose I'm not really the motherly type," said Bernadette. Grace listened to her remove the top from a bottle of hand lotion. She sensed Bernadette's motions as she rubbed the lotion onto one elbow and then the other. She waited for Bernadette to add another sentence. There should be another sentence.

A knock at the bedroom door broke the silence. "Grace, I can't find the jelly," Polly said. "Are you in there, Grace?"

"It was a breeze being pregnant," said Bernadette. She stood up and patted her stomach, flat through the white robe. "Maybe I'll be a better grandma." She walked across the room to the door. "But why would I be? You know what I was? I was a fun girl. Gracie. You got gypped. I love you guys. But you were gypped of a mother." She opened the door. "Your turn, Polly."

Polly entered and Bernadette disappeared into the hallway. "She isn't really a good mom, is she?" said Polly, struggling not to cry. "Sometimes I try to remember that she's pretty."

Grace patted the bed next to her that had been warmed by Bernadette. Polly sat and flung her arms around Grace's neck. As Polly's tears spilled, Grace gave thanks for her sweatshirt. At least Polly wasn't leaking all over her skin.

"I heard Mom say she loved us," Polly sobbed.

Polly seemed to be stuck to Grace, adding an unpleasant warmth, but Grace decided to let her have another minute so that she wouldn't feel rejected by everyone in her life. She counted to sixty in her head as quickly as she could.

"Okay, Pol, let's go."

Polly wiped her nose on her pajama sleeve. "What should we do, Gracie?"

"About what?"

"I heard what Mom said."

"That's not news, is it?"

"But she said she loves us."

"She did say that."

"That's good, isn't it?"

Grace sighed deeply, noting how old and useless sighing made her feel. "Yes, that's good. She said that. But it's how you love someone that matters."

"What does that mean?"

"I don't know. It just sounded good."

Polly wiped her nose on the other sleeve. "Gracie, could I live with you when we're grownups?"

"If I'm dead, that should work out," Grace almost said. But she stopped the words, enjoying them without saying them out loud. "If we don't have to share the toothpaste," she said. "I hate that."

"Okay," Polly replied, as if they had just paid the first month's rent.

"Let's make some dessert for the party now. It's still raining. Maybe we'll make two desserts."

They stood up together.

Nothing was different except that Polly had stopped crying. Grace might have asked Bernadette if she would try a little bit, for Pinky and Beth. If Bernadette knew that she was a crummy mother, she must know what a good one was like. Couldn't she pretend?

She, Grace, could act. She had wanted to say something mean to Polly, but she had let it go and acted as if Polly were a real person. Her heart had made an infinitesimal adjustment, stopping itself before it grew crooked or something.

Crooked. When had Hilda realized that she was beginning to slant the wrong way? And Bernadette? She was as crooked as a parent could be. Did it begin before anyone realized what was happening? Should she worry? No. She might be Hilda-crooked someday, but she would never, ever be Bernadette.

29

The rain stopped early in the afternoon, and the kids trooped over to Frankie's cabin for games. The party, Grandpa Ernest told them, would start at five o'clock because Hilda and Gunda went to bed early.

"I thought this was the party," Pinky said.

"It seems that there are two parties today," said Grandpa. Then he returned to town and picked up Hilda and Gunda. By the time they arrived back at the cabin, everyone else was on the beach.

Grandpa helped Hilda down the wooden steps. Right behind them came Frankie's dad and Gunda, who tried to hold on to Hilda's shoulder as well as her escort's arm.

"Hey, girls," Bernadette called up. "Welcome back to your beach."

Polly huddled behind Chuck, the only person big enough to hide behind.

"Don't worry. Gunda will have a lot of kids to choose from," Grace said to her. "If she decides on Chuck, it should take her all night to lug him from one spot to another."

"Hello, Bernadette!" Hilda said in her high voice when she reached the sand. "This young man must be Charles, the oldest. I remember the other children."

"You're right. This is Chuck."

Chuck stared at Hilda, who looked even odder on the beach than she had in her house or any of the other places Grace had seen her.

"How do you do, ma'am?" Chuck said very slowly.

"Very well, thank you." Hilda smiled sweetly.

"Where am I? Who is he?" Grace whispered to Polly because she was the nearest person.

"You remember my grandson, Frankie, from the park," Grandpa said. "This is my son, Tom."

After everyone including Gunda had been introduced, Gunda stared at Polly. "Girl," she said in her low voice.

Polly smiled a tortured smile at her. "Hi, Gunda," she said, raising her arm stiffly in what looked to be more of an attempt to shield herself than to greet Gunda.

"Such a lovely family," Hilda said, raising her little turtle head a bit higher as she scanned the faces. "Perhaps I should have taken my Gunda out more to play with other children. But I tried to do my best, I truly did." She snapped back to the present. "I can't seem to recall Pinky's real name."

"Patrick," said Bernadette. "His dad picked it. As a matter of fact, I had a name for each kid. But my husband chose a different one for each birth certificate while I was busy turning back into a human being after giving birth."

"What was my name?" Grace asked.

"What?"

"You said that you named us and Dad renamed us. What was my name?"

"Ava. As in Ava Gardner."

Grace. Why had Dad chosen Grace over Ava? Did he like the sound of Grace or did he think that she would bring grace into their lives? Had he considered Catholic grace or the kind of grace that flows effortlessly from elegant people? Had Bernadette ever had grace or simply a lazy way that once passed for breeziness? She would have to talk to Dad about this. He was a good dad. But a lot of things didn't add up.

With wood that the kids found beneath the trees around the cabins, Frankie's dad made the fire. Pinky stayed close to it and added kindling as Mr. Hale instructed. Pinky's eyes looked worse than usual from the smoke, but he didn't appear to be bothered. Everyone ate seated on the sand, except for Hilda, Gunda, and Grandpa Ernest, who had carried folding chairs down the steps to the beach.

"Gunda's not as scary when you can see what she's up to," Polly whispered to Grace. "Or maybe I'm getting used to her." Polly relaxed when Beth sat at Gunda's feet. After

Gunda had finished her hot dog, the coleslaw that Frankie and his dad had made, and a brownie and a snickerdoodle cookie baked by Grace and Polly, Beth let Gunda hold her doll.

While the kids played tag, the grownups talked. Grandpa Ernest announced that it was time to take Hilda and Gunda home when the sun looked about to be yanked below the horizon.

"Bernadette, I hope that you'll bring your family back to the cabin next year," Hilda said, holding Grandpa's arm while Gunda held on to her. "It's so nice to have the families together."

"Maybe we'll make the trek again," Bernadette said. "We're all that's left of the old guard, I guess."

"You're very fortunate to have your children," Hilda said, as though imparting a secret. "I don't know what I would do without my Gunda."

Bernadette followed the departing guests to the steps, then paused and turned around. "C'mon, Bethie. It's time for your bedtime story. You, too, Pinky. Polly, you help me get the kids into their jammies. Chuck, help Gracie clean up."

Beth looked confused. After the initial shock, she followed Bernadette.

"What did she say, Grace?" Pinky said, looking not only red around the eyes but as puzzled as Beth.

"Did you hear what I heard?" Polly said to Grace.

"You'd better catch up, Pinky," said Grace. "Bernadette only reads a bedtime story once in a lifetime."

Grace and Frankie and Chuck cleaned up, and then played catch until the starry night turned into a dark and cloudy one.

"See you in the city," Chuck said to Frankie. "It's been great."

"So long," said Frankie.

Frankie and Grace stayed on the beach. "So he knows that you don't live that far from us, too?"

"Right. It's really no farther than our walk into town. And on a bike, it'll be a breeze."

"My house is a zoo, but you can come over."

"I will. Plus there are movies, and other places we can go to."

Before they walked up the steps holding hands, they leaned together in a kiss that felt as if their dry lips were free-floating away from their bodies. Water lapped in the background but, in the silence, sounded like a roar. Frankie looked into Grace's eyes as if he had forgotten something in them. "I hoped that I'd see you every time I went outside," he said. "I'm going to miss living next door to you."

"Me too," said Grace. She went into the cabin. Chuck's snoring didn't bother her.

30

*I*n the morning, Grace told the kids to look under their beds for lost items. Then they carried their bags of clothes to the car. Bernadette peered into the cupboards and drawers.

"Gad, we're going to have to stop in town for cigs," she said, tucking a box of Sugar Frosted Flakes under her arm and picking up the small bag of extra groceries.

"Can I drive, Ma?" Chuck asked.

"Forget it, Chuck. Remember, no permit? How many times do I have to tell you?"

"I'll probably drive before you do," said Polly.

"Oh, sure," Chuck answered, "and Pinky will fly."

"I think he could," said Beth. "He might."

Pinky turned to Beth with an expression of immense gratitude. How did this sweetness bloom? Those two were still young. Chuck was wrecked. Polly lived in misery much of the time. Was there a chance that the little ones might be normal?

Beth looked at Grace, who was mercifully alone in the back of the station wagon, as they drove away. "Grace," she whispered, "Mommy read to us last night."

"Mommy read to you? Really?" What could she say to Beth? She could tell her friend Margaret that this event rivaled the Second Coming. "What did she read, Bethie?"

"She read a story."

Bernadette would never think of bringing books for the kids. She barely remembered to bring the kids. "Did you and Pinky like the story?"

Beth radiated satisfaction. "Gracie, there was a beautiful lady in it. But she got sick. Then her husband didn't like her."

"Where did Bernadette get the story?"

"*Redbook*," Beth said. "It's a magazine."

Chalk up one for Bernadette, thought Grace to herself. She had tried.

The car swung onto the main road that led to Bagley. "We're leaving cabin country," Bernadette called. "It's back to hot town, summer in the city, after a cig stop."

With the exception of Grace, everyone followed Bernadette into the drugstore, hoping for pennies for the gumball machine or even a nickel each for a candy bar. Grace walked to the end of the block and turned the corner while she waited, leaning against the stone wall.

A short bridge spanned the narrow river several yards ahead.

The bridge arched gently upward. At the high point stood Hilda, rapt, motionless. She looked crushably frail in her print dress, neck sprouting from her chest, hands at rest on the railing. What was she looking at, eyes pulled over the water?

As if tethered to her mother by an invisible rope, Gunda bounced little dance steps in time to a tune that played in her mind. Hilda lifted her hands from the railing and held them out to her daughter. Hands together, they danced to music that only they could hear.

Grace looked away, the intimacy of the image flooding her head. She replaced it with a picture of Frankie at the cabin door. Then she turned the corner and backtracked to the station wagon.

"Grace, Mom bought us all Chiclets! Hurry up!" Polly called from the sidewalk next to the car.

Grace knew that Chuck would open his Chiclets box and empty them into his mouth all at once. Polly would fall asleep with a Chiclet under her tongue and wake up choking on it. Pinky would chew one for the whole ride home and then hide the box. Beth would need help getting a Chiclet out of the box without spilling the rest of them. Then she would clutch her treasure for the entire trip.

"Do you need help, Bethie?" Grace asked.

"Mommy already opened it for me," Beth replied.

"Let's get a move on," Bernadette called to any kids outside the station wagon. The stragglers piled in.

"Will somebody open this pack for me?" she asked, flipping her cigarettes into the backseat while she crashed around in her purse, searching for the car keys. Pinky caught the cigarettes. "And don't let me ever catch one of you lighting up," Bernadette said. "It's a filthy, money-sucking habit. Amen."

"She doesn't want us to smoke cigarettes," Beth said to Grace, "because she doesn't want us to ever get sick like the lady in the story."

"Sounds like a good story."

"And because," Beth added quietly, "she loves us."

"Was that in the story, too?" Grace said, regretting the words as she spoke them.

"No, I just know it," Beth said with a less tentative smile than usual. "Mommies love their children."

"You're right. Bernadette loves you and Pinky and all of us." Grace rested her forehead against the glass that wasn't a window. By choosing the back of the car, she was dependent on everyone else's window for air.

"I have two mommies," Beth continued. "You're my mommy, too."

How could you stand to be a real mom when one little kid with Chiclet breath could break your heart with her goodness and hope in the back of a station wagon driven by a chain-smoking egomaniac? A familiar flicker of rage began to ignite in Grace, but she tamped it down.

Something hadn't been said. What was it? Grace picked up her sister's hand and held it on the seat between them. "I love you, Bethie," she said, aware of never having spoken these words to her.

"What's all the whispering about back there?" Bernadette called. "Are you planning a mutiny?" Bernadette swung a U-turn to head out of town, accelerating down Main Street.

Beth wore a mischievous look. "Mommy, may I drive home?" she called to the front of the car.

"Jeez, Bethie, don't grow up to be like Chuck, promise?" Bernadette said loudly.

Grace squeezed Beth's hand. Bethie was going to be okay. Maybe the rest of the kids would be nearly okay, too.

She trained her eye on a spot down one short block as the car rolled by. From this vantage point, the sun shone in Grace's unshaded eyes. But Hilda and Gunda were visible, if you knew where to look and you looked hard. They stood there still, Hilda and her daughter, her family, now hand in hand, gazing over the water, watching, seeing, together.